OUTSIDE THE LAW

OUTSIDE THE LAW

PHILLIP THOMPSON

BRASH BOOKS

ISBN: 1941298990
ISBN-13: 9781941298992

Published by Brash Books, LLC
12120 State Line #253,
Leawood, Kansas 66209

www.brash-books.com

For my mother, who knows all the words.

ACKNOWLEDGMENTS

A great many thanks are due to the excellent editing team of Lee Goldberg and Joel Goldman. Also, my deepest thanks go to those tolerant few who provided the support, inspiration, and encouragement to keep going: Walt Bode; Grant Jerkins and Eryk Pruitt, whose South is as rough as mine, and who read as well as they write; Joe Clifford and Tom Pitts at the Gutter; Ames Holbrook, raconteur extraordinaire; and, finally, to Brenda, for her patience and tolerance, of course, but mostly for a smile and a gentle push when I didn't even know I needed it—and because everybody needs a little sunshine.

COLT

He climbed out of the car and into the rain falling like silver three-penny nails on a moonless night. Fluorescent lighting bathed the gas pumps in the convenience store parking lot and cast weird splotches of light on the cracked, rain-slick concrete. He pulled on a brown sheriff's department ball cap and squinted at the deputy cars that sat on either side of the pumps, their lights still revolving, slinging blades of vertigo-inducing blue light across the front of the store, which glowed from its windows decorated with neon beer lights.

An engine screamed behind him, and he frowned when he turned to see the local TV station's remote truck pull to a stop by one of the deputy cars. He started toward the store entrance, then spotted John standing near the door over a body—male, facedown, smoke still rising out of a blown-out hole in his back. John saw him, stepped from under the store awning, and met him at the pumps.

He jabbed a thumb over his shoulder in the direction of the TV truck. "Get those assholes out of here," he said.

John turned his head and let loose a piercing whistle that brought a deputy to the door of the store. He pointed at the TV truck, and the deputy—this one in a brown vinyl rain parka with LCSD painted in yellow across the front—trotted over to corral the reporters. He was met by loud groans and a few profanities as they argued with him over the rights of the people and the First Amendment.

He and John walked back to the body.

"Wayne Freeman," John said. "Owner. He was working the register."

He looked at Freeman's body, the longish gray hair askew, his back now a bloody exit wound. His right hand still clutched a semiauto pistol. Nine millimeter from the look of it.

"He hit anyone?"

"Hard to tell in this rain. There's a blood smear here," John said, pointing to the window near the door. "But we won't know whose it is for a while."

He nodded. "What we got inside?"

John scowled. "Two wannabe gangsters—one dead, one beat to a pulp—and one very satisfied Deputy Reynolds."

He winced and, on reflex, glanced back at the TV crew setting up in what was now a steady downpour. "Shit. Why did it have to be the meanest deputy I got?"

"If by 'mean' you mean racist, yeah, makes you wonder."

"Not now, John."

He stepped over Freeman's body and into the convenience store, which was a rat's nest of dry goods, groceries, kiosks of all kinds of shit, fishing tackle, and an array of lottery tickets four feet high behind the register.

Deputy Tom Reynolds stood toward the back, in front of the wall of beverage coolers. Full uniform, of course, thumbs hooked into his gun belt. His eyebrows were nearly as big as his mustache, and he looked like a younger, uglier version of Mike Ditka, if such a thing were possible. Clearly satisfied with himself.

At Reynolds's feet lay a crumpled body that resembled a pile of laundry, except for the pool of blood the size of a trash-can lid that had gathered near the upper half of the torso.

From where he stood, he could tell the corpse was young, black, male. Jeans, high-tops, bright T-shirt that had been yellow before becoming soaked in blood.

Sitting behind Reynolds was another young, black male. Hands behind him, presumably cuffed. Dressed like the corpse, but with a blue T-shirt. His left eye was swollen shut, and his bottom lip was split. Blood had spilled down the front of his shirt like a Jackson Pollack painting.

"Tom," he said.

"Sir." Reynolds always called him "sir" on account of his Marine Corps time, but it still pissed him off. He let it slide.

"What you got?"

Reynolds cleared his throat. "The owner called in a robbery in progress at 2322. I was heading up Highway 69, so I took the call. Arrived here 2331. Encountered a deceased white male out front, apparently shot through and through with a shotgun. I called for backup, but the two perps inside saw me.

"I entered the premises and ordered them to halt so as to arrest them. They were both armed.

"This one," Reynolds said as he pointed to the floor, "decided to take me on. I shot him in the head and a double-tap to the chest. That snub-nose in the blood there is his.

"This one," he said, pointing to the other kid, "is T-Rock. He dropped his weapon. That sawed-off over there by the potato chips."

He looked T-Rock over. Reynolds noticed his scrutiny. "He became combative and resisted my attempt to cuff him. I had to use additional, necessary force."

Bullshit. You couldn't resist slapping him around. He squatted over the corpse and looked at T-Rock, who refused to meet his eyes. "Who's your friend, T-Rock?"

The kid winced. "This is bullshit, man," he mumbled. "This some Dirty Harry bullshit is what it is."

"So, you're telling me you didn't come to rob the place tonight?" He glanced toward the chips and saw the shotgun. Twelve-gauge. Barrel sawed off down to the pump.

Reynolds coughed. "Register's empty, but there's no cash on either of them, so I figure the owner chased one away, probably the one with the cash."

He squinted at T-Rock, who glared back at him, but nodded once.

"Anything else you want to tell us, T-Rock?" he said.

"I ain't saying shit to y'all," he said. "It's bullshit. You got white boys running around robbing motherfuckers and y'all don't do shit."

He stood and stretched his legs. "What are you talking about?"

"C'mon, man," T-Rock said. "Some dude, white dude, from what I heard, decided to take down one them oxy dealers the other night. Ain't nobody looking for his ass."

He smiled and shook his head. "Ain't nobody called in a drug dealer being held up. Hell, maybe we ought to give him a medal. Besides, that shows a lot more balls than knocking over some old man's store."

T-Rock huffed and looked away.

He motioned with his head for Reynolds to follow him. When they were halfway down an aisle, he turned and nearly walked into the huge mustache. He stepped back. "Look, Tom, there's a TV crew out there, so get this kid in a car and back to the station as soon as you can. Don't even look at them. I'll talk to you later about his 'combative' nature."

Reynolds's eyes narrowed, but he said, "Yes, sir," and turned away.

Outside, he had just ducked under the crime scene tape headed back to his car when he heard a voice he didn't want to hear.

"Another shooting, Sheriff?" Craig Battles called.

He stopped. Sighed. Turned to face the reporter. Battles was about his age, with a beer gut and a surly attitude. He had a rain parka on, but the only result it seemed to be having was to direct rainwater onto his notebook, which he was ignoring anyway.

"We'll have a statement for you in the morning, Craig," he said, trying to keep the annoyance out of his voice. "It was a robbery. One of my deputies intervened."

"So you didn't shoot anyone yourself," he said.

You little shithead. "No, I did not, Craig."

"I guess that's a good thing in an election year, huh?" He smirked and wiped rain from his brow. "I mean you've already shot, what, three, four guys in your first term?"

He put his hands on his hips. He felt like shooting Craig Battles. "Look, Craig, you made your point last year with your story about my father. Everybody got what they deserved out of that, all right? Except maybe you. That story didn't land you a job with the *New York Times*, but that's not my problem."

Battles sneered. "Hey, Sheriff, what *is* your problem is the fact—and it is a fact—that there have been several shootings and accusations of excessive violence by your office," he said. "Some folks are starting to wonder if that's the way you solve all your problems."

He leveled a look at Battles. "I can think of a few that could be solved with violence. I'll have a statement for you in the morning." He turned toward his car. "Now I've got enough sense to get out the rain. How about you?"

He flung his ball cap into the backseat and climbed in. Made a mental note to check around about drug dealers getting robbed.

HACK

The land in these parts was different. The terrain he had left an hour earlier was studded with low flat hills separated by wide swaths of rich river-bottom soil spread across flatlands punctuated by pine and oak and woven together by sluggish brown creeks and streams, smaller siblings of the Tennessee River.

He stared through the windshield at this new land—new to his eyes, but familiar to his soul. He caught glimpses of the Tombigbee River, wide and deep, its surface a smooth cobalt blue, as he barreled down the highway headed south. It carved a meandering path not dissimilar to his own down the four-lane highway.

He squinted when he spotted the dull gray Mississippi state trooper car squatting near a rest stop. His eyes flickered to his speedometer and back to the road, and his right hand, of its own accord, slid across the seat to the Ruger 9 mm resting on the passenger seat. His fingers wrapped around the handgrip, drew the weapon to his side, and slid it under his thigh. He drove past the rest area without a sideways glance.

No, the land itself was different, yet at once familiar. Here, the hills in the north gave way to broad rolling prairies corrugated by decade upon decade of farming. Small, nearly forgotten towns of brick and wood buildings slouched at odd intervals on the shoulders of the road, and these hamlets seemed to serve only to break up the monotony of the farmland.

Here, he knew, the people clung to the land and to one another, having long ago flung away hope and dreams. In the hollers and in the feed stores, men sought one another to tell stories, discuss the placement of deer stands, settle debts, or plot vengeance on those who did not. And at the center of all of these discussions, important or happenstance, was the reality of kin. The people here, he knew without knowing a single one of them, were loyal to one another above anything else, save the Almighty. To raise a hand against one was to raise a hand against an entire family and challenge generations-old loyalties oftentimes sealed with violence and blood.

His ancestral land, farther to the north and east by hundreds of miles, the place in which he had originated and from which he had been ejected even as he rejected it, was one such as this. In his land, he had raised a hand against a man, and thus a family. He had left carrying only his name: Hack.

Tonight, he would raise a hand again.

He turned off the main highway onto a narrow macadam road that led into the shady lee of a low ridge on his right. After a few miles, the road ended in another, perpendicular to his route. To the right sat a claptrap one-story general store with a single four-wheeler in the dirt lot. A rusted beer sign took up the entire wall facing the road, the large words and pictures screaming to no one in particular. He turned left. The sun dropped lower off to his right and cast long shadows like lances across the fields of milo and soybeans.

He drove through the countryside in the failing light until only his headlights illuminated his route. He headed generally east, and he met no oncoming traffic, even after nearly an hour of driving, and the land fell away under his car until it approached a smaller river north and east of the Tombigbee. Off to the right, on the near bank, sat a squat white building with a white sign atop a rusted metal pole, illuminated by a single floodlight. The sign proclaimed the establishment as Bill's Bait Shop. He slowed the car and checked the rearview mirror once again for traffic. Seeing none, he slowed further as the car rolled onto the old steel truss bridge looming in the yellow glow of his headlights. The steel girders, painted green like the water below, angled up and across the still river like an erector set. He gazed at the serene riverbanks. The milky light of a half-moon shone on summer vegetation hugging the water's edge, honeysuckle and Johnsongrass, willows arching like delicate fingers over the surface, kudzu blanketing every open space. The water here looked deep.

He drove to the opposite bank and pulled in to the small, battered asphalt parking lot of a two-pump gas station and convenience store. No sign announced the owner, but in the halo of light caused by his high beams, he could see blue paint peeled from the concrete block walls. An ice machine hummed outside the double glass doors. One car, a maroon Chevrolet, sat to the right under a flickering fluorescent light. No customers, though interior lights indicated the store was open for business. The tin roof was painted in red, white, and blue stripes. The decor caused a wisp of a smile to appear on his otherwise grim face.

He pulled to the left of the store, close to the wall nearest the road, and killed the engine. He hefted his pistol and ejected the magazine, then replaced it with another—this one loaded with shells filled with tiny pellets instead of ball ammunition—and replaced it on the seat.

Within ten minutes, he saw the pinpoints of headlights descending the hill toward the bridge, coming from the same direction he had taken earlier. The high beams flashed once, then turned into the bait shop on the bank opposite him. He cranked the car and pulled out, taking his time approaching the bridge.

He stopped his car halfway across the span. He holstered his pistol under his jacket, smoothed his shirt, and checked his tie in the rearview mirror.

The dealer appeared, on foot, at the edge of his headlights, a bulging eight-by-ten envelope in his left hand, smoldering cigarette in the other. He was short and beefy, with a face like a comic-book villain: wide, ugly, and festooned with a scraggly goatee. He didn't appear to be armed.

Hack killed the lights and climbed out. He closed the twenty feet silently, calmly. Nodded once. The dealer nodded back, nervous.

"You would be Robert Pritchard, I presume," he said to the dealer.

Another nervous nod. "Ah, yes, sir. And I got it all—"

He raised a hand. "We'll get to that. First things first."

"Yes, sir," Robert said.

"Robert, you fucked up, but that goes without saying," Hack said in a tone that could have been called friendly under different circumstances. "My employers don't like fuckups. Causes them to question the reliability and competence of their employees. You understand that, don't you?"

Robert exhaled. "Yes, sir, I do. I surely do. But this was a one-time thing. I can guarantee you that. That guy came out of nowhere and jumped me. And I'm here to make it right." He raised the envelope, which shook in his hand. "Double what was stole from me. That was the deal. Four thousand dollars."

He nodded, annoyed at the dealer's groveling. "I see that. But, Robert, there's a couple of things you need to understand. First, there was no deal. That money is your penance, for your sins, if you want to look at it that way. And, second, there's no need to guarantee me anything, because I know this was a one-time thing."

He stepped toward Robert, took the envelope and drew the Ruger in the same motion. He pushed the muzzle into the short man's belly, just under the rib cage and pulled the trigger twice.

Robert's eyes went wide for an instant, then blank as he slumped forward.

He yanked the gun away and let him fall. The body crumpled facedown to the pavement with a dull thud, like a rolled-up rug hitting a hardwood floor.

He stared through the near-total darkness in either direction. The only light for miles, besides the moon, flickered from lightning bugs cruising the riverbanks. He tossed the pistol over a girder and waited until he heard it splash. He bent over the body and went through the pockets until he found the car keys and then pulled the corpse upright by the collar and belt and wrestled it over the steel. He lifted it clear by the legs and let it fall into the river. The splash of the body shattered the stillness of the evening and echoed from the woods.

He peered over the side and watched the corpse sink out of sight, to be borne by the current to a spot somewhere far from this bridge. He checked his sleeve for blood—saw none. He walked back to his car and tossed the envelope on the front seat of his car.

He rolled back across the bridge and, when he neared the bait shop, pulled his phone from his jacket. He punched a button, waited for the voice mail.

"Mr. Lang, regarding the vehicle we discussed earlier today," he said, "it is at the location and ready for pickup. It is a Toyota. The keys will be in the left front wheel well."

He wheeled into the shop's gravel lot and put Pritchard's car keys in place. For two hundred dollars, the driver—a Mr. Lang he had found yesterday on the Internet—had agreed to tow Pritchard's vehicle to a junk car company in Amory, no questions asked. By this time tomorrow, the car would be crushed and stacked with a hundred more in the lot.

He checked his watch. He could still be home by midnight.

COLT

"She was real drunk is what she was." The girl behind the counter was cute, but tired, and not used to talking to The Law. He tried a smile, tried to look less like The Law, more like just a guy. Didn't seem to be working.

She tucked a strand of dyed black hair behind her ear and batted her lashes at him. "I already tole your deputy out there what she did."

"You mind telling me?"

Carla—her nametag said Carla—pursed her lips and looked around the convenience store. Toward the back, where the coffee machines were, a couple of gray-hairs fussed over their cups. Nobody at the sandwich counter off to the right. A teenage boy, tall but slouchy, operated the register on the other side of the counter from Carla, so that his back was to hers. Three people stood waiting for the boy to ring them up.

Nobody stood behind him. He was used to that. People tended to shy away from badges, whether they knew you or not, whether they felt like they had nothing to hide or not.

"Well," Carla said, "like I said, she come in hammered. That was pretty obvious. She wanted cigarettes, of course. You know how drunk people are—they always want cigarettes. It's the damnedest thing. Get drunk, smoke."

He nodded, smiled enough to let her know he was still listening, because he was.

"And 'course, she didn't have enough cash on her. So she had to dig around in her purse to find a credit card. Then when she swipes it and punches in her PIN, and you know what happened."

He arched his eyebrows. "Declined."

Carla nodded. "Yep. And then she went batshit, if you'll excuse the expression." Her blue eyes suggested that she didn't give a damn if he excused the expression or not. "Started hollering that her card was good, she *wants* her damn *cigarettes* and so on. Basically, she wanted me to give her the cigarettes. Like this is some kind of bar she can run a tab at." She cocked her head toward her coworker. "Billy over there called nine-one-one." She laughed, a throaty rumble like distant thunder.

"What?"

"That's when it got real interesting. She lit into your deputy out there in the parking lot. Which was pretty damn stupid, you ask me. I mean, he's huge. Looks like a football player. So, she starts getting mouthy with him, and the deputy is like, 'Ma'am, if you could just calm down,' but she wasn't having any of it."

"You could hear them from in here?"

"I could hear *her*, for sure. Ain't that right, Billy?"

Billy swiveled his head over his left shoulder. "Hell yeah."

Carla nodded. "Course, we could watch it all through the window, too. Anyway, she hauls off and swings that big purse at the deputy, and he blocks it with his arm and spins her around. The bag went flying."

He nodded. "I figured. Saw the stuff scattered out there in the parking lot."

Carla nodded back at him. "Yeah, God knows what all she had in that thing. Your deputy swung her around and basically put her in some kind of wrestling move looked like. Next thing you know, she's cuffed and in the backseat, cussing him to high heaven. That's about when you showed up."

He nodded again. "I thank you, Carla. I'm gone talk to Deputy Carver now. I do appreciate your time and patience."

Carla smiled. "Not a problem, Sheriff."

Outside, Carver sat in the front seat of his cruiser, laptop open. He clacked away on the keyboard. The driver's side back door was open, and two bare feet, toes up, stuck out. Purple nail polish. He peeked around the corner of the door. Around the car, a debris field of lady things was marked with tiny plastic orange cones Carver had pulled out of the trunk. The cones marked off a wallet, some loose change, a pack of chewing gum, a tampon, an ink pen, and a book of matches. The purse from which the objects had flown sat, upright, two feet behind the car.

A mess of blond hair popped up from the backseat. The woman glared at him. She wiggled into as good a sitting position as she could, as her hands were cuffed behind her back. Positioned such as she was, he could see she was top-heavy. The black T-shirt strained against her bosom.

"Ma'am?" he said as neutral as he could.

The woman's eyes went wide and took on a look like a trapped dog. "Sheriff, please, I'm sorry," she said in a voice nearing hysteria or tears or both. His brow furrowed. "I swear to God, I didn't mean to. I'm real sorry. Swear to God I am."

He raised a hand to shush her. "Ma'am, just calm down a little bit."

She pulled her legs into the car and scooted away from him until her back was jammed up against the opposite door. "Nuh uh," she said. Still drunk. Obviously. "I seen what you do to people what cross you."

"Excuse me?"

"I seen you shoot that guy over at the Jug last summer!" she shrieked.

He sighed. He seemed to recall a busty woman in the crowd at the Jug the day he shot O. W. Banks. Who was drunk at the time. Obviously. And holding a pistol in his right hand.

He cut his eyes toward Carver, but the deputy was still clacking on the computer. If he heard the woman—and how could he not—he didn't let on. "John, what's her name?"

"Cheryl Brinks. Missus," Carver said without looking up.

He peered into the backseat. "Well, Mrs. Brinks, I'm not going to shoot you. So just try to calm down, and we'll get this rectified as soon as we can."

Cheryl relaxed. Nodded and exhaled. He caught a whiff of alcohol, smiled anyway. Behind him, a ways off, he heard a faint buzz, a big engine a long ways off. He stood straight just as Carver finished his report, clicked the laptop shut, and then climbed out of the driver's seat. He eased the back door shut, then shook his head and grinned at his boss.

"What?" he said.

"I never tell a suspect I'm not going to shoot him." The grin still there.

"Why the hell not?"

"Makes me a liar if I do."

He chuckled. "Yeah, I suppose so." The noise behind him grew louder.

"I could have saved you a trip into the store."

He shrugged. "You looked busy with Mrs. Brinks there." He waved his hand toward the back of the car and grinned. "And this carefully preserved crime scene. Shit, I thought somebody had gotten assassinated."

"Shut up, Colt."

John stared over his shoulder toward the noise, which had turned into a loud rumble. He turned just as the Ford pickup swerved off the highway and into the parking lot, tires howling on the hot asphalt. Behind the wheel, the driver scowled, cheeks red and angry above the brown beard and below the Bass Pro ball cap.

"What in the hell?" Carver said.

He turned to face the truck, now parked about twenty feet away. "I'm guessing that would be *Mister* Brinks," he said as he started walking toward the vehicle.

"Colt," John said, taking half a step.

He waved him off as he closed on the truck. "I'm good." The driver's door flew open and a heavyset man, fifty or so, piled out. His work boots smacked the asphalt. Jeans, short sleeves. No visible weapon. He knew John was back there, so he just kept walking until he was about six feet from the driver, who stood fuming.

"Can I help you, sir?" he asked. Calm. Professional.

"Sheriff, what is this bullshit about?" The man's hands were visible, but he was clearly pissed.

"I'm sorry. I didn't catch your name," he said.

"I'm Brad Brinks," the man said. "That's my wife you got hog-tied back there." His voice carried across the parking lot to his wife's ears.

"Brad!" she screamed from the backseat. "Go on home, damn it! Don't make thangs worse than they already are!"

Brinks leaned forward, up on his toes like he was trying to propel his voice over Colt's head. "You keep your goddamn mouth shut, you hear! Just shut up!"

Brinks looked back at him. "You gotta put her in cuffs?"

He hooked his thumbs in his pistol belt, the right hand still close to his weapon. "She was being belligerent to my deputy."

Brinks thrust his head toward the cruiser and the debris around it. "You call that belligerent?"

"He does." He stared Brinks down for a second. "You want to keep talking about what I do and don't consider belligerent, or you want to get back in that truck?"

"Look, Sheriff," Brinks said, hands on his hips. "I don't want no trouble."

"Well, you're getting a little right now."

Brinks stared back at him. Steady. Not afraid, but not hostile, either. Just the steady gaze of a man who has won and lost his share of fights, who has taken the measure of more than one man. Eyes of appraisal, like a breeder checking out a pup, seeing bloodlines and potential, strengths and weaknesses, and deriving a full value of the creature before him based on years of experience, good and bad.

"Ahite, Sheriff," Brinks said. "I hear you."

He nodded; Brinks climbed into the truck and cranked up. Headed south on 69, toward Alabama, without looking back.

He watched the truck grow smaller until it disappeared around a curve in the late afternoon glare that bent the orange of the day into a gunmetal gray at the horizon. He was getting tired of this work. Or was he getting afraid—and that was making him tired? No, he was tired of staring down someone in a parking lot or a beer joint or an apartment over something stupid and more often than not induced by alcohol. Cheryl Brinks being the latest example.

Her comment about O. W. Banks rang in his ears. He had already shot three men, killed two. And should have killed the third one just on general principle. Lawman does that, though, and it divides the flock into two groups—one scared to cross you for fear of being shot and the other just looking for a chance to take you down a peg. Brad Brinks was in the second group, but he was smart enough to know today wasn't his day.

He walked back to the cruiser. John stood rigid and ready to draw down, even with the threat gone. "See?" he said. "Told you, I'm good."

John shook his head and grinned. "I shoulda known," he said. "I'm taking Mrs. Brinks in and post a bail, soon as I get all this shit picked up." He swept a muscular arm around to indicate the items on the asphalt.

"Want some help?"

"Naw, I got it."

He nodded, fished his keys out of his pocket. His car was parked off to the side of the store. "All right, then I'll see you back at the office."

"You bet, boss."

He walked to his own vehicle, cranked it, and let the air conditioner start pushing the hot sticky air around the interior before he dropped it into gear and pulled onto the highway.

He took his time rolling up 69 toward Columbus. John would handle Mrs. Cheryl Brinks. Had he not been driving back toward town from the river and heard the radio, he wouldn't have stopped in the first place. He turned the knob on the air conditioner one more notch. His rearview mirror blazed orange, the glare making him squint, and he reached for his sunglasses in the passenger seat. Outside, pine thickets gave the illusion of cool shade, though the lack of rain over the last month meant the gloom beneath their boughs was only slightly less stifling than the sun-splashed wide pastures that fell away from the highway and toward the Tombigbee two miles to the west as he wheeled through a sweeping curve. Overhead, a sky of blue so pale it only hinted at its natural color offered no respite, just wisps of cloud even paler than the sky. Even the kudzu that throttled every fence post and tree and any other stationary object along the highway seemed to gasp for air from broad green leaves withered and fading.

These long spells of dryness, of thirst not slaked, only seemed to amplify the dryness and thirst of the people who lived here. The heat, which even when lacking rain was never without its suffocating humidity, a mocking presence in the air, created a

1 7

need that grew more urgent by the day, a need that transformed into sullen resentment that started deep and burned slowly, only to erupt and rage until it had spent itself.

He barreled past a tiny crumbling cemetery tucked in a stand of oaks, pale worn stone reminders of a long-dead era. The scene brought to mind an image of his mother's delicate frame standing at his dead father's grave, her still-blond head bowed, and her songbird voice carrying the ancient hymn she often sang, "Leaning on the Everlasting Arms." He never could remember all the words, but he smiled at the remembrance of her alto voice and embraced the calm it brought.

He turned off Highway 69 onto a side road, headed north. He picked up the bypass near the Alabama state line to avoid going through town and kept the big Crown Victoria up over seventy-five all the way to the exit for 45 North. He made his way through the traffic and lights for the turnoff to the lock and dam, took it on the yellow light, and drove to the convenience store a mile down the road on the right.

He sat in the car with the engine running, watching the activity in the store through the plate glass window front. Two other cars in the lot. The old blue Honda belonged to Burton; the Chevrolet must belong to the teenager standing at the counter while Burton rang him up. He waited until the kid exited carrying a huge cup with a straw sticking out the top. The kid unlocked the Chevy with a remote, cranked up, drove off.

He climbed out and met Burton at the door. He grinned. Every time he saw Jim Burton, he thought of John Lennon. Same circular little glasses, long hair, long face. Burton looked like 1969 when it got old.

Burton didn't smile back. He rarely smiled at him. "Sheriff." Burton stepped aside as he came through the door. "What's up?"

"Relax, Jimmy," he said as he walked to the counter. "I'm just here to get some Copenhagen."

Burton looked skeptical. "That all?"

"Pretty much. How you been doing?"

Burton walked back behind the counter, pulled a can of Copenhagen from the rack on the rear wall, slapped it on the counter. He shrugged. "I been doing OK."

"No trouble from that McNairy bunch?"

Burton had gotten crosswise with a group of Tennessee redneck mafia types about a year earlier. The group had set him and his store up to run a food stamp scam, a clear violation of Burton's parole terms—part of his sentence for his possession conviction. But Burton, being just smart enough to see an opportunity but not smart enough to cover his tracks completely, had gotten caught skimming profits from the group, who liked to call themselves the McNairy Mob. Realizing his impending fate, Burton did what any good parole violator would do—he began cooperating with the authorities. Burton had been his main informant ever since, especially after he had had to shoot Kenny Jenkins in a parking lot not far from here because of the scam.

"No trouble at all," Burton said, sliding his hands in his jeans pockets. "Fact is, I ain't heard from them since…you shot Jenkins."

He nodded, slid a ten across the countertop. "That's about what I figured. But you hear anything else around town lately?"

"Like what?"

"Like anything. Names, deals coming and going, things like that."

Burton's eyes narrowed behind the glasses. "Deals? What's your angle, Sheriff?"

He put his hands out, open, as if to show he had no subterfuge in mind. "I don't have an angle, other than I'm the law. And come to think of it, that's a pretty big angle. But I got a kid in my jail from the other night talking all kinds of shit about somebody ripping off drug dealers."

Burton shrugged. "Ain't heard nothing about anything like that."

"Really." He gave Burton a long stare while he slid a thumbnail under the paper label of the snuff can and sliced it open. "Nothing at all?"

Another shrug. "Naw. I ain't in the business anymore, remember?"

"This kid in my jail," he said, "he's looking at armed robbery, accessory to murder at the least. DA wants to charge him with capital murder."

Burton shook his head. Kids these days. "Sounds like he's in deep shit."

"The deepest. And a guy like that is willing to roll over on just about anybody. Know what I mean?"

Burton frowned. "Yeah, I know what you mean, but like I said, I ain't heard nothing. At all."

He stepped back. "Fair enough. Keep an ear out, Jimmy. You hear anything about a guy, a white, guy, ripping off dealers in any of your social engagements, you let me know, ahite?"

Burton nodded. "Yeah, sure."

He left Burton standing behind the register with a confused look on his face. He sat in the car and scolded himself for thinking he was tired earlier. He wasn't tired. He was just bored.

DELMER

He eased the car into a parking spot on Forrest Street and cut the lights. Downtown was dead this time of night—a little after midnight—so he didn't worry about being seen. From his car, he could see up to the apartment on the second floor. Lights on in the window, softened by a gauzy curtain. Behind the soft light, strobes of white and blue and shadows. TV still on.

All right, then, we wait.

He felt better about this one. This was already going better than the first job. He called it a job, not a heist, like this was some kind of movie. It was a job. And a damn serious one.

The first one, three weeks ago, had been a first-class clusterfuck, he could admit to himself now. The dealer, a barfly turd named Robert Pritchard, had pulled a fast one on him.

Bad enough he'd had to spend nearly twenty dollars on beer at Winnie's while keeping an eye on Pritchard. He'd scoped him for a few days, checking out his ride, if he was carrying, if he kept money on him. He drove—when he drove—a used Lexus, didn't carry a piece, and kept a wad on him.

So, at Winnie's it was a simple matter of waiting until Pritchard had enough gin and tonics or whatever the fuck he kept buying and walked out of the bar and across the street toward his apartment one street over. Which he finally did after about three hours.

He watched Pritchard leave, then finished his beer, and stepped out. He pulled a baseball cap low over his head and tied a bandana around his face. Easing up to him through the dark had been easy enough. Pritchard was short, overweight, and drunk.

Looking back, he realized that had been amateur shit, something out of a bad western. Still, he got the drop on Pritchard as he cut through an alley between a downtown bank branch and a closed discount store.

He bull-rushed Pritchard up against the wall, figuring he could slam him against the damp bricks hard enough to daze him while he grabbed the cash. But he didn't count on Pritchard being cat-quick. They'd crashed together against the wall in the dark, Pritchard drunk but still with plenty of fight. He wasn't carrying a gun, but he yanked a blackjack out of a back pocket and swung at his head. It smacked him a glancing blow that stunned him for a second and caused him to stagger a little.

He got his shit back together and gut-punched Pritchard, then head-butted him back, slamming the back of Pritchard's skull against the bricks. That had rattled his ass good. He jammed a hand into Pritchard's pocket, yanked out the wad, and reached around to his hip pocket and grabbed his wallet. Then he threw an elbow across Pritchard's nose just for good measure. He hauled ass out of there, sprinting down the sidewalk and into the tiny, dark veterans park across the street from the bank. He ducked behind a tree, made sure Pritchard wasn't on his ass, and then shot through the trees to his car. Got away clean with two grand. He couldn't believe a dope dealer would be foolish enough to carry that much cash on him.

He watched the window until the light clicked off, around one thirty. Checked his watch.

Give him twenty minutes, then get it on.

Rick Munny lived in the apartment. Was in the navy, but now was dealing across half the county, probably the half Pritchard wasn't selling to. But Munny didn't walk around with cash on him, near as he could tell, so that meant he had to keep it at home somewhere.

He checked his gear: short-handled sledge in the passenger seat, in case the door gave him any real problems. The pistol, a snub-nosed .44 Magnum, was loaded up with hollow points in a holster on his left hip so he could do a fast cross draw if he had to. He'd opted for a rubber Halloween mask—one of the pullover types, a zombie or something ugly as shit and badly painted—instead of the ball cap and bandana routine. In his T-shirt pocket was a hotel key card he'd use to work the lock.

He glanced around the street. Still dead. He grabbed the sledge and the mask and slipped out of the Mazda, easing the door shut behind him. He crossed the black street and quick-stepped up the iron stairs, stepping over the one that had creaked the day before when he was scoping the place out, and faced Munny's door. Locked. He smiled and slipped the mask over his head, felt the July heat close in on him immediately.

Who the hell decided to make these things out of rubber?

He worked the lock with the key card, felt it give, and opened the door just enough to slip inside. Shut the door soundlessly behind him.

The living room was dark as a cave.

I can't see a goddamn thing.

His eyes wouldn't adjust. He slid a foot forward, trying to feel where the wall, any wall, was so he could find a reference. His foot bumped something—the couch? A chair? He froze.

An overhead light flashed on, scalding his retinas and nearly blinding him as Munny charged out of the bedroom, screamed, "What the fuck!" then pulled up short at the sight of a zombie holding a sledgehammer.

His eyeballs recovered just in time to catch, from the corner of his eye, a blur coming at him from around the bowling-pin shape of Rick Munny. His brain kicked into gear fast enough to recognize a wild woman, wearing only a T-shirt, flying at him with an aluminum baseball bat and taking a mad swing at his head.

He pivoted just enough to catch the blow on his shoulder and snapped the sledgehammer out, popping the woman square in the knee. She went down like a stone in a howling pile of hair and legs, shrieking profanities. Her caterwauling distracted Munny long enough for him to draw the .44 and point it at Munny's disbelieving face.

"Your money. All of it," he said.

Munny was not a tall man, but he stood up as straight he could. "Are you nuts, you son of a bitch?"

"Do I look nuts?"

Munny cocked an eyebrow. "You're wearing a goddamn zombie mask and beating on my girlfriend with a sledgehammer. Yeah, you do."

He thumbcocked the revolver. "Now. I ain't got time for long conversations."

"It's in the bedroom," Munny said, his hands now raised, even though he had not been so ordered.

"Back in there and get it. I'll follow you."

Munny obeyed and pulled two stacks of bills out of a nightstand. Handed it over. "Here. It's ten thousand. That's all I got."

He snatched the cash out of Munny's hands and crammed it into a back pocket of his jeans. His shoulder was starting to hurt. He backed away, toward the front door.

"Do not even think about coming after me," he said.

Munny shook his head. On the floor, his girlfriend writhed, hands clasped around her knee. "Hey, fucker," she hissed. "You broke my leg."

He looked down at her, gun still leveled at Munny. "Serves you right."

He stepped out of the apartment, pulled the door shut, and shot down the steps. Sprinted to his car, dove in. Checked the apartment as he cranked up, then took off down Forrest, lights still out. He flicked them on two blocks later at a red light.

Ten grand. Not a bad night's work. But, shit, that bitch clocked me.

COLT

"Technically, ma'am, I haven't decided to run for reelection, but I do appreciate your support," he said into his desk phone as John walked into his office carrying two mugs of coffee. He nodded John into a chair as he took the Marine Corps mug.

"Yes, ma'am," he said as he took a sip.

John smiled and drank from his own Chicago White Sox mug.

"Yes, ma'am, and thank you very much for calling," he said. "You, too, ma'am. OK, good-bye."

He hung up and huffed out a breath. Took another sip of coffee.

"Technically?" John said.

"Oh, you heard that?"

John chuckled. "Yeah."

"That was Mrs. Ruth Ann Weathers, and she believes that what this country needs is stronger laws," he said, shaking his head. "And she'd be mighty proud to support my reelection campaign."

"But, technically..." John said.

"Hey, I never said I was running."

"Never said you weren't, either."

He leaned back in his chair. "Yeah, well, I don't want to make a hasty decision."

John furrowed his brow. "What's the matter, Colt? You know you could get reelected easy. People 'round here like the fact you keep things in order."

He shook his head. "I don't know about that. Last year or so was pretty rough, and you can bet that asshole Craig Battles won't let people forget it. Last night being the latest case in point."

"Screw that," John said. "You know what people think of the press in general—and Craig Battles in particular. And yeah, last year was rough, with Rhonda's boy getting killed."

"And the people I shot," he said, draining his mug.

John nodded. "People who needed shooting for the most part."

"And my father," he said.

John set his mug on the floor and crossed his arms. "Colt, look," he said. "Most people don't care one way or the other about the way your father went out. That may sound harsh, but you know it's true. Hell, you said yourself that most of these folks just thought of him as a town drunk, anyway. And Craig Battles can write all the stories he wants about a murder that happened fifty years ago, but you know as well as I do that, had your father not settled the matter, you would have arrested him and charged him. Let that shit go, man."

"Easy for you to say," he said.

"You think so? You think it's easy being your deputy through all this shit? Remember, I'm the one got an ear shot off."

He rolled his eyes. "Fuck you. It was only half an ear."

John laughed, grabbed his mug and stood. "Yeah, yeah. Easy for you to say. Want more coffee?"

He nodded and handed over his mug. "How's Rhonda doing?"

The question stopped John in midstride. He turned, a mug in each hand. "She's fine. I'm going to see her tonight."

"She still looking for another job?"

John nodded. "Yeah, and I don't blame her. Being a court reporter after you buried your only son? Hasn't been easy on her."

"I know," he said. "I worried about her for a while after Clifford died. Even after we put Bennie in jail."

John nodded. "I know you did. And don't worry, I'm taking good care of her."

"Did I say anything?"

"You didn't have to."

John turned for the door, but Becky stepped in from her dispatch desk, a worried look on her face.

"What's up, Becky?" Colt said.

"Looks like we got a floater. On the Luxapalila. Some guy in a boat just called it in."

He was up and around his desk before she stopped speaking. John looked at him, asking a question with his eyes.

He shook his head. "I'll take it," he said, then turned to Becky. "We know where exactly?"

She nodded and glanced at the yellow sticky note in her hand. "Guy said about a quarter mile up from where the rivers meet on the south bank, right there where the Luxapalila park is now."

"He still there? The boater, I mean," he said.

"Far as I know," Becky said.

"All right, I'll head out there. Call Freddie Mac and tell him to meet me."

"You got it, Colt," Becky said and walked into the outer office.

"And tell them not to touch anything," he yelled after her. She waved a hand in acknowledgment.

He looked at John, shrugged. "Probably a drowning."

"I don't recall any missing persons reports being filed," John said.

He shrugged. "Could have just happened. Or somebody could have filed a report with the city police. Either way, won't know until I get out there."

———

Ten minutes later, he wheeled the Crown Vic to the grassy side of the blacktop road that ran along the banks of Luxapalila Creek, and stopped in the only open spot along the two-mile length of the road.

He walked down the gentle slope to the muddy brown creek's edge. Except for the sluggish current of the creek, the area was as still as a tomb. Overhead, the sun blazed, and the glare off the water's surface made him squint, even with his eyes shielded by sunglasses. He looked left and saw a fishing boat sitting low in the water, a solitary man standing amidships, about fifty yards away.

The fisherman must have spotted him at the same time, because he started waving his hands, then leaned over and hit his horn—two short toots.

He walked quickly down the bank, keeping an eye out for snakes, and saw the corpse through the tall grass at the water's edge. The fisherman pointed at the body, and he nodded.

"Hidy, Sheriff," the man said when he got within earshot. He was tall, with a goatee surrounded by a three-day growth of salt-and-pepper beard, and wore a NASCAR ball cap.

"Hey," he said, swiping his brow with the back of his hand. "Are you the one who called this in?"

The man nodded. "Yes, sir. My name's Eddie Price. I was coming downstream, headed toward the river." He tossed his head toward the Tombigbee, about a quarter of a mile downstream. "I just happened to be looking in that direction. You know how you scan the banks as you head down the river."

He nodded. "Sure. Ahite, then, let me take a look. Just hold what you got, you don't mind."

"No, sir, not at all," Price said.

The body was facedown in the grass. Jeans, T-shirt, one tennis shoe missing. Short guy, little heavy. The arms were purplish and pruned. Dark hair matted and tangled with leaves.

He surveyed the immediate area. No mashed-down grass or footprints around the body. Up the bank, trees lined the road. He looked back at the thick mud on the bank. No drag marks.

He squinted at Price. "This how you found him?"

Price nodded, his sunglasses glinting in the sun. "Yes, sir. Couldn't tell what it was at first, but I saw the sun reflect off of something, I guess that watch there on his wrist. I made another pass and got closer, saw it was a body and called your office."

"OK, then," he said. "I'm going to need you to hang tight until my coroner gets here, and then I'm going to need your statement back at my office."

"No problem, Sheriff."

He heard Freddie Mac before he turned to see the coroner stomping through the grass toward him, photographer in tow. Freddie Mac's face was the color of a ripe tomato, and he wheezed like an old-timey steam engine as he hauled his overweight frame along the bank.

He put his hands on his hips and watched Freddie Mac snap a pair of latex gloves over his wrists and produce a blue bandana from the leather attaché case that seemed to always be draped from his right shoulder.

"Freddie Mac," he said as the big man pulled up next to him.

The coroner mopped his brow with the bandana and nodded. He cast a sharp glance at Price, who seemed unsure of any protocol in such a situation and just nodded back.

"Hey, Colt," Freddie Mac said. "What we got?"

He leaned his head toward the body. "Looks like a drowning that washed up right here."

Freddie Mac scoffed, which pissed him off. "We'll see," he said.

"Yeah, see for yourself. No drag marks from the edge or down the bank. No grass disturbed."

Freddie Mac nodded, and then knelt by the corpse with a loud exhalation and a grunt. The photographer, some new kid with a mop of red hair, began his vulture-like ritual of circling the body, snapping pictures with the same intensity and accuracy as a sniper.

"You touch anything?" Freddie Mac asked.

"Didn't have time before you got here," he said to Freddie Mac's wide back.

Freddie Mac plucked a wallet from the dead man's hip pocket and held it up over his shoulder. He took it and checked out the driver's license.

"Robert Pritchard," he read aloud. "Aberdeen address. Five foot eight. Hundred sixty pounds." He took another look at the corpse. "That was about thirty pounds ago." He tapped the license photo, thinking. *I don't know this guy, right? But why does the name strike me?*

Freddie Mac grunted.

He went through the contents of the wallet. Eighty dollars cash, a Visa card with the same name. No photos. No membership cards. He looked over at the corpse. Not dressed for fishing.

"What was that, Freddie?" he said.

"Nothing much," the coroner said. "From the lividity and the pruning of the skin, I'd say he's been in the water at least a couple of days. Skin ain't started to separate much—that usually takes about a week before it starts. Hard to tell right here, of course. Here, help me turn him over."

He squatted beside Freddie Mac and grabbed a leg. They rolled the body over.

The face was still intact, pretty much, and more or less corresponded with the image in the driver's license photo. But what really caught his attention were the two gunshot wounds to the chest, near the heart. The holes, pulpy and leaking water, were surrounded by dark bloodstains that looked nearly black against the blue T-shirt on the body.

"Well, that makes things a little more interesting," Freddie Mac said.

He leaned back on his haunches, and thought of the last homicide victim he'd pulled out of the water. That had been Clifford Raines, Rhonda's boy. He shook off the memory and stood, figuring the thought of that made Pritchard seem familiar. He faced Price. "Mr. Price, you can go now. We'll take it from here. But I'm going to call my deputy, John Carver, and he'll be in touch with you real soon, y'hear?"

Price, who seemed shaken by the sight of a dead man's face, nodded and hit the ignition switch on his boat. The outboard roared to life, and he steered away from the scene without another word. He turned back Freddie Mac, who stared at the body with a puzzled look.

"What's up?" he said to the coroner.

"Looka here," he said. "These gunshot wounds. What they look like to you?"

He bent over and stared. "Dunno. Nine millimeter, maybe?"

"Yeah," Freddie Mac said. "Exactly. Nine millimeter means high-powered. More often than not you get an exit wound. But I didn't see any exit wounds on his back side. Did you?"

"No," he said.

Freddie Mac heaved himself to his feet with a grunt that seemed to echo across the creek into the pines beyond. "Just seems odd," he said. He pulled his cell phone out of a pocket of his black polyester trousers. "But I guess we'll figure it all out in the autopsy." He punched a number on the phone and put it to his ear. "Yeah. Y'all bring the bag on down here, and let's haul this guy out." He ended the call and gave a thumbs-up to the photographer, who slung his camera and started walking up the bank toward the coroner's van.

"Anything else, Colt?" Freddie Mac said.

He shook his head. "But let me know about the autopsy." When the two men from Freddie's shop had made their way to them, bagged the body, and hoisted it for the walk back, he followed them up the grassy slope. He drove off wondering about Freddie Mac's puzzlement.

HACK

He drove slowly down Elvis Presley Boulevard toward downtown. Traffic was light, even though it was a workday morning, and he took his time. He had spent the night, or what had been left of it by the time he'd gotten back from Mississippi, out of the city, in a hotel in Germantown, east of the city.

He hated Memphis, and this morning that hate complemented his already dark mood. He came to town only when he had to, which was whenever his employer, a man named Franklin Brooks, wanted him to. Lately, Mr. Brooks had required his presence more and more often. That displeased him.

He entered the city and immediately absorbed the gloom he felt around him in the crumbling neighborhoods, the heat, the inertia, the lassitude of a city that, for all appearances, seemed on its last legs. Mr. Brooks's downtown office sat high above the city and its grime and desperation, and it offered sterile views of the Mississippi and the bridge leading into Arkansas, the Peabody Hotel, and the new baseball stadium. From his aerie, Brooks and his people could feel safe and distant from the malevolence and angst below. But down here, the hopelessness took hold like the razor wire and window bars on neighborhood businesses and even houses that might have once been homes.

This was not his place—out in the open, glaring asphalt spaces, and concrete shadows. He preferred to remain in the hills to the east, the hills that reminded him of his native Kentucky. In the woods and ravines he could remain an entity, a wraith both feared and revered, his judgment and wrath known by word of mouth, whispered about in the farms, hideouts, and small beat-down towns.

He steered the car through the narrow city streets and into the parking garage at the bottom of the building housing Brooks's office, found a spot, and took the elevator out of the dank concrete cavern

The door pinged open, and he stepped into the carpeted corridor toward the double glass doors that led to Mid-South Capital Investments. The receptionist, a severe-looking older woman with silver hair and clunky black-framed glasses, spoke in low tones into the phone tucked between her shoulder and right ear. Her penciled-in eyebrows shot up as he entered the lobby, and she indicated with her eyes for him to go to Brooks's office.

Franklin Brooks sat behind a simple wooden desk with his back to a wall of glass that presented a God's-eye view of downtown Memphis. He clicked the door shut behind him, glanced around the spacious office toward the dark leather couch and low table, and finally to the man himself. He stood several feet from the desk and remained silent, holding a bulging white envelope in his right hand.

He never could figure out Brooks. The man wielded a startling amount of power and wealth, yet seemed to deny it in everything he did. Nearly everything. The office was spacious and comfortable, but hardly luxurious. The leather couch and table to the right were functional, not stylish. His desk could have come from any big-box store in the city, and its only decorative touches were the various documents scattered across the top, a camouflage-patterned coffee cup, and an ashtray that was clean except for the paper band of a cigar.

He knew Brooks had served in the army at some point many years ago, during the Vietnam era, but saw no evidence of the man's service or patriotism on display on the walls. Instead, shelves filled with books on subjects from the Civil War to import laws lined the walls.

The only evidence he could see of Brooks's fortune was in his appearance. There, it seemed, the man spared no expense— today, he sat comfortably in a charcoal-gray suit, perfectly tailored. Armani, he guessed. Blinding white shirt, pale blue silk tie, full Windsor knot. Plain but elegant cuff links—the gold looked brushed.

Even at seventy—he guessed the man to be just shy of that age—Brooks still had a full head of white hair that he combed back and wore longer than most men his age, but it worked for him. His pale face and small nose wore few wrinkles, giving him an eternally boyish look accented by blue eyes set in deep crow's feet at the corners, the only hint as to his real age.

Brooks finished writing on the document in front of him and looked up. He pressed his lips together and gazed at the envelope.

"Good morning," Brooks said.

"Morning, sir."

"That was a hell of a lot of work for you for four thousand dollars. I trust that's the amount in there." He nodded at the envelope.

He placed the money on the desk. "Yes, sir, it is. And, yes, sir, it was. But the lesson will go a long way, especially over there."

One side of Brooks's mouth went up. He leaned back in his tall leather chair and looked him in the eyes. "Normally," he said, "I'd agree with you on that." His brow furrowed.

"Normally?"

"Yes, normally, something like this happens, we deliver a... lesson, as you call it, and everybody falls into line."

"I'm not sure I understand."

"Usually, another one of our associates doesn't get robbed before you can deliver the lesson."

They're fucking drug dealers, he thought. *Just call them what they are: little dirtbags that sell your dope so you make shitloads of money.*

He raised his eyebrows. "Sir?"

Brooks leaned forward on his elbows. He frowned. "The other night. Another one of our people—Rick Munny, something like that—got robbed by some idiot in a Halloween mask. Broke into his apartment in the middle of the night, beat the shit out of his girlfriend with a sledgehammer, pulled a gun, and made off with ten thousand dollars."

He cleared his throat and voiced the thought that jumped to mind. "What the hell was the dealer doing with ten grand in the house? And how did this thief know there was that much?"

Brooks shook his head. "Don't know that he did. And I don't know why Munny had that much cash on him. Granted, these guys aren't the brightest."

"But still."

"But still, nothing," Brooks said. He sat up in his chair. "The point is that we got robbed again. I don't like getting robbed, Mr. Hack. Your job is to ensure that we don't."

He stared back at the man who employed him, paid him well, and gave him a great deal of latitude without asking a lot of questions about how he went about his jobs. Franklin Brooks was interested in results. And money. *His* money.

"I understand that, Mr. Brooks."

Brooks stared at him for a full thirty seconds, and then shook his head. "I don't know what the hell is going on down there, but you better get a handle on it. This is the same damn county where the sheriff shot Kenny Jenkins a while back. God knows what that little shit said before he got killed."

"I'm working on that," he said. "I've made contact with some of Jenkins's…associates in the hope of learning who might be doing this."

"Doesn't seem to be helping so far," Brooks said, this time with an edge in his voice.

"What about this sheriff?" he asked.

"What about him?" Brooks said.

He shifted his feet, sensing an opportunity. "If he managed to turn Kenny—or any of his associates, for that matter—he may become a problem."

Brooks sighed. "If he becomes a problem, then solve it. Again, that's why I hired you."

"I'll take care of it," he said.

"Please do," Brooks said, "because, meanwhile, some dipshit in a zombie mask is ripping off my people." The words came out of his mouth like a bitter lozenge, foul and unwanted. "And don't come back to Memphis until you do."

He met Brooks's eyes. "Sir?"

Brooks's gaze was like ice. "Hack, as I just said, your job is to ensure this doesn't happen, whether it's a sheriff interfering in our business or some little redneck shithead ripping us off. It's the only reason you are in my employ. And well paid. One time is an anomaly. Twice in a month is enough to cause me concern about the validity of my investment. Not to mention the business with that other...that other incident."

"That was an unfortunate and singular occurrence, I can assure you."

"You think that makes it OK? An apology? Jesus Christ, man, you burned down an entire house in downtown Knoxville to cover your tracks! That was your best course of action?"

He glanced away, at the bookshelves, loathe to endure the hysterics of a man who had never seen the bloody business end of his empire.

"Couldn't be avoided," he said, looking back at Brooks. "The girl had so contaminated the room when she got free that it would have required a prohibitive amount of time to sanitize it."

"You mean clean up the blood."

"And other things, yes."

Brooks stood, his face a crimson mask of fury, and pointed a finger at him. "Goddammit, Hack, I've just about had it with your flowery words and your goddam airs. That shit in Knoxville cost me more money that it made. You are on thin ice with me. You should take this as an opportunity to redeem yourself. Otherwise—"

"Otherwise what, sir?"

He thought Brooks might have a stroke.

"Otherwise," Brooks said in a trembling voice, "you will end up in that river out there with a bullet in the back of your head. Now get out of my office."

He felt his eyes narrow. He formed a thought, swallowed it. He said, "I understand, Mr. Brooks." But the old man had already dismissed him and returned to the documents on his desk, as if he'd never been in the office, or even alive for that matter.

He left without another word. He passed the bitter bitch at the front desk with a nod and rode the elevator to the street, where he stepped into the gut of Memphis: hot, humid, loud, and confined. The air and the street sticky. The morning rush hour traffic clattered by, the cars creating vortexes in their wakes, spinning fast-food wrappers, newspapers, and programs from the baseball stadium down the street. He grabbed his phone from his jacket pocket and punched a number. The kid answered on the second ring, as he turned left on Union and passed Huey's store on the way to the Peabody.

"'Sup, Mr. Freeze?" Dee said.

He stifled the urge to swear. He didn't like Dee. At all. But the boy was useful, primarily because he was a young black male in the drug trade. And greedy. Thus, very useful.

"I thought we agreed, Dee, that the only way to address me was by my last name," he said.

"Sorry 'bout that," Dee said, sounding not at all contrite. "Jus' tryin' to, you know, have a little fun. What do you need?"

He stepped through the revolving door into the ornate lobby of the Peabody Hotel. "I need you to be ready to go to Mississippi as soon as possible."

"Mississippi? The hell is in Mississippi?"

He stopped, closed his eyes. "Dee, I'm not paying you ask questions. Am I?"

"No, sir."

"Good. I will call you tonight and tell you where to meet me. We're going to be gone for a few days."

"How soon we leavin'?"

"I'll let you know. And while you're at it, put that phone of yours to good use and see what you can find about the sheriff in Lowndes County, Mississippi."

Dee was silent for a beat. He knew the kid was contemplating disappearing, weighing his options, counting his money. "You got it, Hack. Whatever it is, I'm sure you got your reasons."

He hung up and walked to the hotel elevator. *What it is is exile. I've been sent away. But I will be back when this is done, and Brooks will regret his condescension.*

His anger rarely rose quickly, and it did not now. In due time. He was vain about the cultivation of his wrath, honed and cured over a lifetime, like a gardener tending rare orchids. He wore his wrath as a mask of silent menace, a cruel countenance that harbored neither mercy nor negotiation. In due time.

The thought reminded him to call the guy in Nashville regarding the now vacant safe house. He would have thought the guy would have been better at getting blood off the walls. He didn't want to have to burn down another one.

COLT

When he opened the door to his office, the last thing he expected to see was himself.

But there he was, in a foot-tall black-and-white photo that looked so stern yet friendly that he thought it could easily be mistaken for a mug shot. Except that it took up the entire left half of the yard sign.

He sighed. *Goddamn reelection campaign.*

"Becky," he said, still staring at the boxes piled high on his desk and attempting to avoid eye contact with himself. "Who ordered this shit?"

Becky looked up from her dispatch desk, pulled the earbud out, and wrinkled her brow. "Well, Colt, you did."

He turned to face her. Her face a question mark. She'd gotten her hair cut, even though it was still long enough for the blond ponytail that had become a fixture in the office. Her hair looked nice, and he knew he should say something complimentary, but he never did, because he never knew what to say or how to say it without sounding like a complete ass, so he let it drop.

"I did?"

Becky nodded and tried to suppress a smile. She couldn't. Her brown eyes danced.

"When in the hell did I do that?"

"About a year ago," she said. "During a staff meeting, which, if memory serves, was probably the *last* staff meeting. I brought it up and said you needed to start thinking about your reelection campaign. As in starting your reelection campaign. You grumbled something about money being tight, and I told you how much you had left in the campaign fund and that I could get you some signs made. You said OK. Election's in nine months, you know."

He huffed, recalling absolutely none of Becky's recollection, but not doubting a word of it. "I did, huh? Well, all right, then. But unless I also redesignated my office as the storage room, can we get them moved out of here?"

Becky folded her hands on her desk. "As soon as Joe Ray gets back from traffic duty."

He nodded and stepped into his lair. Rigged up the fancy coffeemaker to brew a cup, and stared at the boxes while the machine wheezed and spat, generating an almost real cup of coffee.

The disarray unsettled him. The office wasn't much, but it was his. The only view from the window behind his chair was the old cemetery. The government-issued furniture reminded him too much of the Marine Corps, and not in a good way. But inside this dim, still space, he could be alone if he chose. In his own sanctuary. Not much of one, but his, thanks to the voting public and government funding. And he guarded it like a fierce monk.

The last thing he wanted to think about was a goddamn reelection campaign. He wasn't even sure he wanted to get reelected. His mind wrestled that slippery thought until he sat down with his coffee to read through the morning e-mails, notices, and alerts. He was halfway through his inbox when Becky appeared at his door.

"Colt. John's on the radio. Said he needs you."

He jerked his head around the computer. "*Needs* me? What's up?"

She shrugged. Had she been wearing green and red, she would have made a pretty good Christmas elf. "Didn't say."

He sighed. "Well, where is he?"

"Steens."

He rose. "All right. Tell him I'll call him on his cell on my way over."

She nodded and disappeared.

John answered as he was pulling out of the lot and roaring down old 82, the big Crown Vic bucking over the puckered asphalt of the ancient two-lane.

"This better be good, John," he said, already grinning. Wasn't like John to call him for help.

"Oh, you're going to love it," his deputy said. "You remember that bank got hit over in West Point two days ago?"

"Yeah, I remember. Somebody got away with all of seven hundred dollars."

"Well, we got him."

He one-handed a hard left and hit the gas, screaming north up a county road toward Steens. He hit his lights and siren, knowing the intersection coming up at the top of the hill a mile to his front. "Yeah? OK, so arrest his ass and bring him in. You didn't need me for that."

"Oh, I didn't say we'd arrested him yet. You'll see when you get here."

He slewed the car through a zigzag turn at Highway 50 and nearly went airborne as he crested the highway. The Dixie Auto Parts store blurred past as he barreled onto Gunshoot Road and over the Luxapalila bridge. He blew past the Steens Superette, a squat gas station at a T intersection that was truly the last vestige of the hamlet. Even at eighty miles per hour, he felt a pang of nostalgia for the long-gone and forgotten cotton gin and school that looked like ancient ruins when he was a kid. Progress, he thought, erases just about everything.

About a quarter mile ahead, he saw blue lights flashing from two of his cars on either side of the road. Doors open, noses pointed toward a third car, a red Honda, on the right-hand shoulder. Driver's door also open. No human activity discernible.

"Colt, watch it," John yelled as he killed the engine and climbed out. John was ducked behind his vehicle, he could now see, weapon drawn. The new deputy, Moore, squatted beside him, hat off, Marine Corps Reserve haircut glistening in the too-hot sun.

He crouched and ran to the car. Slid beside John, who was all business. He knew from firsthand experience that this was not good for whomever or whatever was in the other car.

"What you got, John?"

"You ain't going to believe this shit."

"Try me."

John nodded. "OK, so dumbass over there—" He jerked his head toward the red Honda thirty yards to the front. "Robbed the bank in West Point couple days ago. He's flush with cash, right? Well, today dumbass runs out of gas. Walks to the gas station up the road there, pays for five gallons with a hundred, store clerk recognizes him from the news, calls nine-one-one. Chris and I get here about the time he finishes refilling the tank."

He nodded. "Dumbass is right."

"Yeah, well then he pulls a piece—revolver—and cranks off of a couple of rounds as we're getting out of our vehicles," John said. "He empties the cylinder—and *now* he wants to talk. I want to shoot him just on general principle."

He looked at Deputy Moore, whose expression indicated he did not approve of talk about shooting a suspect, principles or not.

He put his back against the trunk and stretched out his legs. "OK, so now what?"

"Well, now he's talking shit."

"He's got to do something. He's out of ammo."

"That's what I'm thinking," John said.

"What's this guy's name?"

Deputy Moore perked up. "Calvin Bibb, sir."

John grinned down at the Glock in his hands. Colt caught it, gave John a look. "Thanks, Moore. All right, I'll see what Calvin Bibb has to say."

John shifted, already working into position to cover him. "Watch it, Colt. He's been talking crazy, and not just from this goddamn heat."

He raised to a squat. "Aren't most bank robbers crazy anyway?" He stood and yelled over the car. "Mr. Bibb! Calvin Bibb! This here is Sheriff Colt Harper. Thought I might have a word."

"Sheriff, got dam it, I done tole them deputies I ain't going in without a fight!"

He looked down at John and Moore. Both nodded.

"You didn't tell me that," he said to John.

"Sorry, boss," John said as Moore looked on, horror-stricken. "Musta got caught up in all the excitement."

He sighed. *Sometimes this job is a pain in the ass.*

"Calvin," he called out. "I understand you're a little bit upset at the moment. But you know I have to take you in. You robbed a bank and, besides just being plain against the law, it's a federal offense, too. And there's three of us, one of you, and you're out of bullets, I believe."

Silence. Humidity bore down on him; highway glare hurt his eyes. Staring at Bibb's car, he said, "John."

"Gotcha, boss."

"Mr. Bibb," he said to the Honda, "I'm going to take that as you agreeing with me. I'm coming up there so you and I can talk like civilized folk without all this yelling in this heat, you hear? I am armed, and I will not hesitate to shoot you if you try anything, you hear me?"

Silence from the car. His anger flashed. He drew his .45 and marched toward the Honda.

Bibb popped up from behind the driver's door and into his front sights. He was older than Colt had reckoned, at about fifty or so. Short with short salt-and-pepper hair that looked like it hadn't been combed in at least a month. His mouth worked furiously, but no words came out. His nose and eyes were too big for his face, making the workings of his mouth even more comical. He froze at the sight of the .45.

"Calvin," he said, still walking with the pistol leveled, "show me your hands. Right now."

Something in Bibb snapped. He jumped two feet straight up and screeched, a caterwauling so piercing it actually scared him. He stopped, momentarily stunned, his brain scarcely registering the gas can in Bibb's right hand. It hurtled toward him, tumbling through the air. On reflex, he adjusted and fired. The round tore through the metal and howled off into the thick air. The can landed two feet in front of him and rattled to a stop in the gravel.

Bibb bolted across the pavement and down the steep shoulder, short legs bearing him away as fast they could. Still stunned, he stared in something nearing amazement. Then his senses returned.

"Well, shit," he said. "John, I'm going after him." He didn't hear the reply. He holstered his pistol and took off after Bibb.

For all his dramatics, the short man hadn't gotten very far. He closed the distance to Bibb across the pasture, forgetting he was an officer of the law, or being watched by two of his employees. He broke like a wide receiver down the sideline, head down, arms and legs pumping, going deep, outrunning his coverage until he was five yards from Bibb, who wheezed and made a strange mewling sound as he ran out of steam.

He launched himself and laid into Bibb with a shoulder, hitting him like a linebacker with a clean shot at the quarterback. The smaller man collapsed like a cardboard box, hit the grass hard, face-first.

He was on Bibb a second later, pushing his face farther into the dirt as he snatched Bibb's wrists and cuffed him. Read him his rights with sweat and grit dripping off his nose and chin onto the back of Bibb's head.

John and Moore appeared, weapons drawn on either side of the prone Bibb. He pushed himself to his feet and looked at his deputies, shook his head.

"You ain't going to believe this shit," John said between breaths.

"Try me," he said.

John grinned over the top of his pistol, still pointed at Bibb. "We found the money in the backseat."

He laughed. Had to. "All of it?"

John nodded. "Every dime. Well, minus gas money. Six hundred and ninety-five dollars."

"But he ran out of gas," he said. He shook his head and reached over, snatched a snuffling Bibb to his feet and pushed him toward the highway. "Calvin," he said, "I swear to God, you must be the dumbest bank robber I ever met."

Driving back to the office, he recalled his earlier sense of unrest, the day John arrested Cheryl Brinks, the mountain of campaign materials in his office, and now a murder.

He didn't want the job anymore. The realization surprised him and didn't, all at the same time, like slowly but certainly understanding there is no Santa Claus. He didn't know what he wanted yet, but it wasn't this. Arresting drunk women at convenience stores, chasing idiot bank robbers through cow fields, and dealing with murder victims. Or trying to justify to the public why his deputy shot somebody during a robbery.

He was still fondling this new yet familiar realization in his mind as he walked through the office doors and Becky stood. He kept walking toward his door.

She followed him into his office. "Colt," she said as he rounded his desk. "Freddie Mac called and said he was finished with the autopsy on that guy y'all pulled out of the river. Said to give him a call; he had some information you might want to take note of."

He sat and shot her a glance. "He said that—'information I want to take note of'?"

"Exact words," she said. "I wrote it down. Want to see?" She shoved the sticky note at him.

He waved her off. "No, no, I'll give him a call. Tell John to come on in when he gets back."

"Will do," she said. "We can talk about your campaign later."

"Yeah, a lot later."

"Don't be that way with me, Colt. You know I'm not going to forget."

He held up his hands in surrender. "Believe me, Becky, I know you won't forget."

She spun on her heel and strode out of his office. He picked up the phone receiver and punched in Freddie Mac's number.

"What you got, Freddie?" he said when the coroner came on the line. He opened a drawer and rummaged for a pen.

"Well, it's a homicide, of course," Freddie Mac said. "But you knew that already. You remember, I thought it was a little weird there was no exit wound? Did the autopsy, now I know why."

He drummed his fingers on the desk. Sometimes County Coroner Freddie Mac Baldwin could be a royal pain in the ass with all the dramatics of his job, which weren't very much, but he really liked to make the most out of them.

"Well?" he said.

Freddie Mac chuckled. "Your victim didn't have any exit wounds because he was killed with two rounds of nine-mil snake shot to the heart."

He grunted and wrote "*Snake shot?*" on a notepad. "Kinda strange way to do it," he said.

"I thought so," Freddie Mac said. "I'll leave motive and what-not to you law enforcement boys, though. Looks like he'd been in the water three, four days, like I thought, and was most likely dead before entering the water."

"Hmmmm," he said. "Snake shot makes getting a ballistics match impossible."

"Yes, I s'pose it does," Freddie Mac said. "Like I said, that's law enforcement stuff."

"Thanks, Freddie Mac."

"Anytime, Colt."

He hung up and stared out the window, trying to discern a reason for Robert Pritchard's demise. The sound of John's footsteps crossing the hardwood floor broke his reverie.

"You rang, boss?"

He swiveled his chair to face John, who stood with several sheets of paper in one hand. "Yeah, you got something on our vic?"

"Was working on it before we got the call on our bank robber." He held up the papers. "Pritchard has—had—two priors for possession and a DUI. First possession was for weed six years ago. That was simple possession. About four years ago, he got busted for possession with intent to distribute—oxy—but that got pled down by your favorite public defender to simple possession."

He shook his head. "Yeah, Gideon's a silly bastard, but he knows his way around a courtroom." He told John what Freddie Mac passed along about the gunshot wounds.

"So what are you thinking?" John asked.

He stood and walked to the window and gazed at the cemetery across the street. "My gut says it was a hit. Shot like that, most likely somewhere else, then tossed in the current to float away from the scene. But what I can't figure out is why somebody would waste time on a low-level nobody like Pritchard."

"Dunno," John said. "If it *was* a hit, maybe he just pissed off the wrong supplier. Or dopehead."

He turned to face John. "Yeah, maybe. The other thing I can't quite figure out is why his name seems familiar to me. Hand me that file."

John handed it over, and he flipped through the pages until he found the arrest sheets. He stopped on one page that held a statement Pritchard had given.

Well, what do you know about that?

He looked up at John. "I'm going to read through this. Let's nail this down as fast as possible. I can already see the headline the paper's going to run on this one."

"You got it, boss," John said, then walked back to his desk.

He leaned against the window, studying the aged stones below. Whatever Pritchard did, it earned him a gruesome death. He sat at his desk and read through the statement Pritchard had given after his second arrest, the one for distribution. It was a fanciful tale, full of the usual bullshit of "it was my grandmother's prescriptions" and "I had no idea those pills were in my car" and other usual lame-ass excuses. But Pritchard must have either been scared, stupid, or a real asshole. Or all three. He had no problem naming names, and one of those names was Jim Burton.

Jimmy, you lying little shit. I could run your ass back to Parchman before the sun comes up.

Rick Munny was the other name. He'd heard rumors ever since he'd gotten elected that Munny sold dope all over the county. That rumor was reinforced in the statement he read now and further confirmed by the comments made by the arresting officer, a Deputy Armstrong who left the office with the old sheriff. Armstrong noted that Munny was suspected of selling oxy for the McNairy Mob, that half-baked bunch of rednecks who fancied themselves a crime syndicate. Armstrong cited several other "unverified witness accounts" as to Munny's role as dealer.

He closed the file, turned to his keyboard, and tapped in Munny's name in the database. Sure enough, there he was: name, photo, address, rap sheet. Former navy, gunner's mate. Living in the county for ten years. Arrests for drunk and disorderly, public intoxication, speeding tickets.

Doesn't sound like a redneck mob dealer.

He wrote the address down and exited the database.

He walked through the office, past the dispatch desk. "Becky, I'll be back," he said to the top of her head.

———

Ten minutes later, he knocked on Rick Munny's apartment door. When it opened, Munny's eyes went wide at the sight of his badge.

"Mr. Munny?" he said. Smiled.

Munny recovered and narrowed eyes. "Yeah, that's me. What seems to be the problem?"

"You mind if I come in, Mr. Munny? I just need to have a word."

Munny's demeanor changed, and he knew this conversation was not going to go well. "I don't mind at all, Sheriff, as long as you got a warrant."

"I don't need a warrant, Mr. Munny, to have a conversation."

"'Bout what?"

"Fella name of Robert Pritchard."

Munny shrugged. "Sorry. Don't know him."

"Really. Seems you knew him at one time. Enough to be named as a 'known associate' of his about four years back when he got popped for possession with intent to distribute."

"What?" Munny said. He smiled and shook his head. "Nope, not me. You ought to talk to him about that and let him know he's got his facts wrong."

"Well, normally I'd do that, but seeing as he's laying on a table in the morgue with a bullet hole in him, he ain't saying much."

Munny's eyebrows shot up.

"Yeah," he said. "Deader'n shit."

"That's too bad, Sheriff," Munny said. "Really is. But I don't know nothing about that or anybody named Pritchard."

He heard another person in the apartment. Over Munny's shoulder he saw a woman limp through the living room. She was wearing very short shorts, with a knee brace on her left knee.

"Hey, Rick, who's that?" she said.

Munny cut his eyes over his shoulder. "Don't you pay no mind," he said. "I'll be in there in a minute."

"Aw, come on, Rick," the woman said as she hobbled toward the door. But then she caught a glimpse of the badge on his shirt and stopped. "Oh," she said. She turned and disappeared down the hall.

"That looks like a bad knee she's got there," he said. "She all right?"

Munny frowned again. "Ah, she's all right. She, uh, fell not long ago. Busted her knee up is all."

"Fell, huh?"

"Yeah, she's clumsy."

"You know, Mr. Munny, I wonder if we have a domestic abuse situation here. I mean, I wouldn't know of course until I searched the premises and interviewed the lady there. Normally, I'd need a warrant, but if I decide what I've observed constitutes probable cause, I could do that right now."

Munny stared at him for a solid twenty seconds, then stepped out onto the walkway and clicked the door shut behind him. "Look, all right, I knew Pritchard. I mean we weren't drinking buddies or anything, but I knew him."

"Through your drug dealer network, that it?"

Munny exhaled and shook his head. "I, uh, knew he sold pills, yeah. And what I heard was he got ripped off not too long ago, but I don't know jack shit about him getting killed."

"Ripped off? By who?"

"Hell if I know. But the rumor going around—the one I heard—is that some asshole wearing some kind of Halloween mask did it. Crazy little shit."

He watched Munny's eyes dart back and forth. "But just ripped off? Not killed."

"Nope. I heard ripped off."

"You hear about any other dealers being robbed?"

"Uh, no," Munny said. Eyes darting again. "Just him. But, hey, you know how folks talk, right? Who knows if it's even true?"

"Oh, I know all about how folks talk. That's how your name always seems to come up when people start talking about dope dealers in this county. I was you, Mr. Munny, I'd start being careful. You never know who might be watching your ass."

Munny nodded. "You right about that."

"All right, then," he said. "I appreciate the conversation. You stay out of trouble, you hear?"

"Yes, sir." He eased the door open and disappeared inside.

He walked to his car, and called John on his cell. "Hey, start squeezing the snitches," he said when John answered. "I think there's somebody running around robbing some of the dealers in the county."

"Really? What makes you think that?"

He filled John in on his conversation with Munny.

"So," John said, "you think Munny is lying?"

"He's lying about something. Maybe he got robbed, too. Or maybe he robbed Pritchard and killed him."

"I'm on it," John said.

MOLLY

For the fifth time in twenty minutes, Special Agent Molly McDonough reminded herself to put in for a transfer as soon as possible.

She sat scowling at her computer in her cubicle at the end of one of three rows on the floor. Her location put her adjacent to the main aisle on the floor and at an angle to the break room, which allowed her to hear the goings-on in there. At the moment, the goings-on consisted of three male agents discussing a particularly festive weekend in downtown Memphis, the city six floors below them.

She focused on the spreadsheet on her screen. It was her own creation from a year ago. She had taken the bureau's Bomb Arson Database, known in the Bureau of Alcohol, Tobacco and Firearms as BATS, and tailored it specifically for the state of Tennessee by rewriting and adding code. She had included several entries that were based on her own experience as a field agent and that were specific to the state of Tennessee. It had taken her six months to convince her bosses that it was both legal and worthwhile. It paid off within two months of her introducing it to the Tennessee field offices and the state's own bureau of investigation. After three meth labs blew up in the hills of East Tennessee over a six-week period—all of which had initially been ruled as cases of meth cookers not knowing what they were doing—she'd gone to work.

Turned out a rural drug lord was eliminating all his competition by hiring ex-military men with explosives experience to blow the labs up in a way that would seem like an accident. It almost worked. But Semtex is easy to spot, if you know what to look for and you have the resources to do so. She'd been able to home in on the drug dealer within two months, which, in her estimation was too long, but the best she could hope for, since she had to coordinate with the fucking DEA, which was nothing but a pain in the ass.

The case had earned her a little bit of fame in the Tennessee BATF offices—and had gone a long way, she hoped, at redeeming her name.

Which was about to take a hit again if the three clowns in the break room didn't knock it off and get back to work.

She closed out the database and decided to check the news digests, since it required less thinking on her part. She pulled her dark red hair back into a ponytail, huffed out a long breath of annoyance and scanned the headlines of the stories selected by someone—she never knew who or where—to distribute to all ATF offices in the state. Usually, the stories she read were not new to her, having set up her news app on her phone to look for even more specifics than those offered in the digests. Today's collection was mostly low-level stuff, robberies, break-ins.

But one item caught her attention. A suspected drug dealer had been shot and killed, his body found on the banks of a small creek, a tributary of the Tombigbee River, in Lowndes County, Mississippi. In other words, she thought, in the middle of nowhere. Well, drugs belonged to the DEA. Those cowboys could probably figure that one out in about six months or so.

She lifted her coffee cup to her lips. Cold. She sighed, yanked her smart card from the computer and headed to the break room. She'd have to endure the festive boys up close. At least she wasn't wearing a skirt today.

She elbowed her way past the men, all dressed business casual, sleeves rolled up, service weapons on hips, and moved toward the counter to put her cup under the spigot.

"Hey, Molly, you might appreciate this," said one of the men behind her. She recognized the voice. Courtney Gaddis. "You like all kinds of odd data."

She didn't know whether Gaddis meant it as a compliment, but she didn't really care, either. "Not if it has to do with how many beer cans you can crush before your hand cramps," she said.

The other two men snickered as Gaddis rolled his eyes. "You been eavesdropping on us?"

She sipped from her mug, grateful to have a hot refill. "Eavesdropping? I could have heard y'all down on the street."

Gaddis ignored the comment. "Anyway, you hear about that druggie got shot down in Mississippi?"

"Read something about that just now in the news clips."

Gaddis nodded. "DEA buddy of mine was telling me the guy was shot twice, in the heart." He jabbed a finger just under his rib cage. "But get this. The shooter used what they call snake shot, they think. Weird, huh?"

One of the other two, Williams, wrinkled his brow. "Snake shot? You mean that stuff people use to shoot rats with?"

Gaddis nodded, and Molly said, "Snake shot around here. You can buy it at any Walmart. I don't know if it's all that weird. Country folks around here shoot snakes all the time, maybe the shooter's gun just happened to be loaded with it."

The men nodded. Gaddis took a mug from the counter. "I suppose," he said.

"Or," Molly said, "maybe the shooter wanted to make it so ballistics wouldn't have anything on him. But I'd bet on the first one."

She stepped past them and back to her desk. Pulled up the dead drug dealer story again. It *was* weird. Drug dealers don't accidentally get shot twice in the heart. Which means it was a hit. Which means the shooter *meant* to use snake shot on the hit.

Strange. And now my Spidey sense is kicking in.

JOHN

H e checked his watch and swore at himself. He should have left twenty minutes earlier, when he knew Rhonda would leave her office. By the time he made it over to the courthouse to break the news to her in person, and gently, she had left for the day. And her car wasn't parked at her house when he'd sped over there.

Now, he was cussing himself and playing a hunch as to her whereabouts. He drove through the downtown streets shaded by oaks and magnolias, past antebellum homes that stood like tired aristocratic old southern ladies, past the huge stone and steel hulk that was once the marble company, but now only an ancient skeletal pile of debris and a roosting place for animals, the home-less, and addicts.

He wheeled through the cemetery gate, turned right on the first gravel path, and saw her standing, her head bowed, arms across her chest. Swearing again, he slowed to a stop.

She turned her head toward him as slammed the door and walked to her.

"Rhonda," he said as he put his arms around her, and she buried her head in his shoulder. "Hey, I'm sorry."

She sniffed and wiped tears from her cheeks. "How did you know where to find me?"

He stroked her back and stared at the headstone of her son's grave. "I intended to leave early today and tell you about the... about the guy we pulled out of the river. Before you read about it in the paper or saw it on the news. I went by your office and your house, and when I didn't see your car, I figured you heard and this is where you would go."

She looked up at him. "You did?"

"I did."

"Why did you want to tell me?"

"So this wouldn't happen. Or even if it did, I just figured you didn't need to do it alone."

She stepped back from him and gave him the saddest smile he'd ever seen, one that made his heart sink and leap at the same time.

"That's what you said at the funeral."

"What's that?"

"You told me you came to the funeral because that was something you didn't want me to have to go through alone."

"It's still true. I don't want to see you alone."

She heaved a sigh. "Thank you, John." She turned again to Clifford's grave.

He fell in beside her and took her hand in his. "You're welcome. You OK?"

She shrugged. "I don't know. Most times, yes. But other times, no, not at all. Even though it's been a little more than a year, it feels like it was yesterday. I overheard a couple of the clerks in the office talking about…that, and, I don't know, it all came rushing back, and I felt like I was being crushed from the pain all over again."

He squeezed her hand and silently chastised himself. "I'm sorry, Rhonda."

"Don't blame yourself, John," she said in a soft voice. "You're here now, and I'm not alone. That's all that matters. I haven't been alone for a year because of you."

He put his arm around her and held her as the day's sun bled away into the pines at the edge of the cemetery.

HACK

Rick Munny was a very stupid man.

Despite being trained by the military, the man knew absolutely nothing about security. His number was in the white pages. He made no real effort at discretion, swaggering around town with a woman ten years his junior, a woman with a penchant for drunkenness and running her mouth. And absolutely no morals, if the stories were to be believed. And he had no reason to doubt them. He'd seen the woman—Carla—three nights earlier in a barbecue joint at the edge of town. She wasn't with Munny, but she wasn't alone. Or sober. The two leering fools who kept feeding her drinks could barely contain their amusement or their carnal desires, as their hands frequently slid up her bare legs under her skirt. She made no effort to cross her legs or stop them. The brace on her left knee was a convenient excuse not to, he reasoned. He had finished a plate of ribs and fries as he watched the spectacle, which ended only when the trio hustled out to a Dodge in the parking lot.

Tonight, it was Munny who was alone, sitting in the cab of his pickup truck at the end of an unremarkable gravel road in an unremarkable corner of east Mississippi near the Alabama state line. At least the man could follow directions.

He rolled to a stop behind Munny's truck and killed the engine. He looked over at Dee. The boy's face was a mask; the insouciance, he knew, was carefully practiced and altogether artificial. He reached for the .32 revolver between them, hefted it, and slid it into a holster under his left arm. Dee's eyes followed his movements, but he didn't speak. Didn't betray a thought or doubt.

"Stay here," he said.

Dee raised an eyebrow, nodded. He stared through the windshield.

The day's heat had broken in the failing light, but the gravel still burned through the soles of his shoes as it crunched underfoot. The wind slithered through the boughs, pushing the humidity away ahead of a storm and turning the pines into whispery schoolgirl gossips. Cicadas and bullfrogs sang from the dark, their melodies sharp and crisp, but brief on the breeze. Sounds would carry a long way on the thick wind tonight.

He took his time, savoring the collapse of another day and the slowing and dimming of life and its sounds, smells, moods, and frenzy. Munny climbed out of the truck as he approached, slammed the door, and put his hands on his hips, a scowl making even uglier an already unhandsome face. Tattoos on the arms sticking out of the T-shirt. Jeans hanging loosely around legs, seemingly too spindly for his bulk. His appearance was not in the least repentant.

He stopped a few feet from Munny and addressed him: "Mr. Munny, it's good that you are on time. You may call me Hack."

Munny lowered his head and arched a brow, as if he'd just heard a language he did not understand. "OK," he said with the slow pace of the uncertain. "I have the money."

He raised a hand. "We'll get to that. Though, I have to admit, I'm surprised that you were able to come up with the required sum in this amount of time. You do have it all, correct?"

Munny sighed. "No. I do not have it all, Mr...Hack. I have *some* of it. I'd say I have most of it."

He clasped his hands behind his back. "I see. Well, as I said, we'll get to that."

Munny snorted through a disgusted look. "Look, I'll get the rest of it; that's not the problem."

"Oh? That's not the problem, Mr. Munny? Please enlighten me as to what you believe to be the problem."

Munny crossed his arms over his belly and glared at him. "The problem is that shithead who stole my money. What are we doing—what are you doing about that?" He spat into the darkness creeping into the road.

The arrogance of the man might have been impressive under different circumstances, he thought. But different circumstances these were not, and Rick Munny's arrogance, compounded by his stupidity, only raised in him a sort of clinical curiosity, as if he were watching him from afar or through the glass in a laboratory.

"Excuse me, Mr. Munny?" he said. "*Your* money? Clearly your grasp of the organizational structure that employs you is lacking. As is your ability to understand your role in it. The money that was stolen wasn't *your* money. It belonged to someone else. It would be more accurate to say that you *lost* someone else's money. Furthermore, the person who stole it—and what I am going to do about that—are none of your concern. None of your concern at all. Do you understand that, Mr. Munny?"

Even in the flat gloom of evening, he could see Munny's face darken. He drew the .32 and shot Munny through his right eye before he could speak. The shot echoed through the woods, borne away on the wind. He walked to the now supine Munny, studied the mutilated face and pulsing blood like a sculptor, and shot him through the left eye. Again, the report of the bullet caromed through the pines.

He holstered the weapon, then fished Munny's keys from his pocket. He took a small gym bag from the front seat—"most" of the money.

Dee stared at him through the driver's side window, his face registering only a hint more interest than before. "You didn't say you was gone shoot the guy."

He smiled. "You didn't ask. Here. Drive his truck back to his apartment and park it. I'll pick you up at the 7-Eleven on the corner. Don't speed, and don't do anything stupid." He tossed the keys across the seat. Dee slid out the other side without a word.

COLT

He headed down Old 82 toward Lake Lowndes, and the susurrus of the tires on the hot asphalt and the familiarity of the route caused an ache that reminded him he'd never enjoy the ride to the lake the way he had most of his life. Not since the day he drove to the spillway to find Rhonda's only child, Clifford, facedown in the rushing water, half his head shot away. He hadn't been back since.

He wouldn't have come out today had it not been for Becky's insistence that he make an appearance as "the incumbent, and, more importantly, the man the people of the county trust to keep them safe." He wasn't sure if he was really trusted—nor was he sure he was keeping anybody safe.

But since Becky had told everybody who had anything to do with the big fish fry the Lions Club was putting on, he had no choice but to put in an appearance.

He pulled to a stop near the main boat landing and bait shop, grateful he was as far away from the spillway as possible. To the left, on the slope that led down to the small, weathered fishing pier, a crowd of about fifty men and women mingled around a line of grills fashioned from fifty-five-gallon drums. The charred grates were loaded with fillets and whole fish beneath heavy clouds of greasy smoke. He pocketed his cell phone, walked toward the crowd, and put on his best Sheriff Smile.

Sweaty grins from the men met his own, and he noticed more than a few come-hither looks from the women, who, even in the late-afternoon heat and grill smoke, managed to look poised and as coquettish as forty-something wives of Lions Club members could be.

He nodded and grinned his way through the gauntlet of outstretched hands and "Hey, Sheriff, good luck in that election" wishes until he stopped at the metal washtub full of ice and longneck beers at the end of the grill line. He figured he'd accept a little off-duty hospitality from his constituents, and he didn't have to wait more than twenty seconds before Larry Wilkerson put an ice-cold bottle in his hand.

"Sheriff," Wilkerson said. "Thank you for taking the time to come by. We know you're a busy man, and this means a lot."

He clinked bottles with Wilkerson. "Thanks, Larry. Glad I could make it. 'Preciate your support."

Wilkerson, originally from up around Tupelo, had taken a small inheritance from his father—a soybean farmer—and turned it into a small but profitable sheet-metal company with a plant out near the airport. Divorced, remarried to Cindy McPherson. Wilkerson played the part of a local mogul to the hilt: country club tan, stylish haircut for his still-thick salt-and-pepper mane, just-right YMCA gym physique, all wrapped up in ostrich skin boots, chinos, and an expensive blue dress shirt, tailored, of course. Not a drop of sweat on him.

"Read the paper about that fella y'all pulled out of the Lux," Wilkerson said. "Terrible thing."

He nodded. "Even for a drug dealer."

Wilkerson cleared his throat. "Uh, yes, I suppose. I was just saying reckon that'll keep y'all busy for a while."

"Yes, it will." He wondered if Wilkerson meant he would be too busy to look into whether his son was still selling weed to his buddies, but he let it go.

Cindy appeared at Wilkerson's side, her own country club tan highlighted by a pale yellow sundress that seemed to serve as a reminder that she was still fit and curvaceous. Her auburn hair was tied back with a yellow ribbon, and she smiled at him with both her prim mouth and her blue eyes, just as she had when they'd gone to high school together.

"Well, hey, Colt," she said. "Thought I saw you walk up."

He saw her husband cut his eyes at her.

"Hey, Cindy," he said. "I'm just stopping by to say hi, shake some hands."

"Well, all right, then," she said. "You got my vote, you know that."

He tipped his bottle. "And I thank you."

His cell phone vibrated in his pocket, and as he produced it, he held up a hand to the Wilkersons. "Y'all excuse me?"

Larry all but twirled his wife away and into the crowd.

"Yeah, John, what's up?" he said as he gazed at the sparkling blue surface of the lake.

"Got another body, Colt," John said. Just a little bit of excitement in his voice.

"Where?"

"Somewhere off 182, Old 82, as you call it. Becky said Bishop's Bottom or something like that."

"Yeah," he said, already walking back to his car. "I know where it is. Where are you?"

"Headed south on 12 about a mile from the city limits."

"Meet me at South Lehmberg and Old 82, right there at the city line. You can follow me from there."

Twenty minutes later, John's car followed his off the highway onto a gravel road he knew by heart, one he'd first driven as a teenager. Bishop's Bottom was a dark, spooky fen with a gravel road shortcut between the highway and the road to New Hope. It also had a reputation for being haunted, with mysterious noises and sounds and boogeyman sightings going on for years, mostly by teenage boys in an attempt to frighten their dates into their arms. It rarely worked, he recalled.

He flew down the narrow trail and over a low rickety wooden bridge that spanned a tiny, sluggish creek and stopped short of a deputy's marked car and a green Ford pickup. A uniform stood with two men, who seemed to be telling a story with their hands while the deputy took notes.

John ran up to him as he stepped out of his car.

"Goddamn, Colt, you trying to get me killed?" John said, running a hand through his hair. "You driving this narrow-ass road like you a bootlegger running from the feds."

He was already walking toward the deputy. "Take it easy, John, I know this road like the back of my hand."

"Of course you do," John said, louder than necessary. "But I don't."

"I'll keep that in mind." He pointed. "Go check that out. I'm going on up ahead."

The deputy had already cordoned off the scene with crime tape about ten yards beyond the two vehicles.

The body of Rick Munny lay supine on a dirt turnout nearly invisible from the main gravel road. He ducked under the tape and approached the corpse. Two sets of tire tracks. Different vehicles. Munny's arms were outstretched, hands empty. No gun in sight. His face looked like a grotesque jack o'lantern, both eyes gone and replaced by black, bloody holes. Flies buzzed around the edges of the flesh. He knelt and examined the eyes. Gunshot, no doubt. He looked at the black dirt around the body, but saw no brass. He considered turning the body over, but thought better of it without Freddie Mac there.

He felt John come up behind him. "It's Rick Munny," he said over his shoulder.

"One of the dealers who got ripped off recently? You know him?" John said.

He stood, hands on hips. "Yep. Well, I don't know him personally, but I did talk to him the other day, after I read through the Pritchard file. Pritchard named him—and that sorry-ass snitch Burton—in his statement. I pressed him at his apartment, and he told me he knew Pritchard got robbed, but not much else."

John looked at the body. "Well, he ain't going to say shit now. Shot his eyes out. Interesting. Think it's the same guy who did Pritchard?"

He surveyed the gloom of the trees, which blocked out nearly all sunlight and cast the area in a weird greenish-yellow tint. "Hard to tell. Two shots like before, medium caliber. Doesn't look like any exit wounds, but I ain't touching him before the coroner gets here." He pointed. "Near water—that's McCrary Creek through there, runs into the Lux closer to town. You notice the tire tracks?"

John nodded. "Two vehicles, looks like."

"That's what I'm thinking," he said.

He started walking back toward the deputy, and John fell into step beside him.

"These two guys just happened across him, which I think is bullshit," John said.

"Why?"

"That little road there is damn near impossible to see if you're driving."

He stopped in the gravel. "They're probably out here shooting squirrels. And probably are worried about not having hunting licenses. But press them anyway. I'm going to visit Burton again and make sure he's not holding out on me. And make sure I get Freddie Mac's report the minute it's complete. I want to know if Munny's car keys are on him."

John nodded. "You got it, boss.

MOLLY

She made her way down the corridor as quickly as she could after a lunchtime workout in the gym on the third floor. She preferred to work out in the morning, before the small weight room filled up with testosterone. The early morning gave her plenty of time to get a decent circuit with the weights and a good workout on the bike and still have time to shower, dress and be at her desk before most of the other agents came in.

But she was having a day. Thanks to the ankle-biting yap dog in the apartment across the hall, she'd barely slept. Ergo—she said the word always with sarcasm—she didn't hear the alarm. Already late, the car in front of her at the gas pump was apparently being driven by the world's stupidest human. At the gym, she realized she had forgotten to throw clean socks in her bag. And, twenty minutes ago, she'd stepped out of the shower to discover a broken hair dryer.

So she scowled and marched to her desk with wet hair, her shoulders hunched, silently daring one of the men to say something—anything—so she could shoot him.

She flung her gear under her desk, powered up her computer, and willed the coffee machine to make her cup as fast as mechanically possible.

Halfway through her first of several cups, she came across an item in the morning mail that made her forget her bad luck so far. A suspected drug dealer, Richard R. Munny, had been found in some woods in east Mississippi with his eyes shot out. She pulled up Google Maps and confirmed her thought—second dead drug dealer in as many weeks in that general area. The report stated that Munny had been shot with what appeared to be pelletized shot from a handgun. Close range, no sign of struggle. Tire tracks indicated two vehicles at the scene. She pushed her cup to the side of the desk, adrenaline momentarily replacing caffeine.

Snake shot again. Is somebody sending a message?

Intrigue gripped her, but concern, too. She had thought little of the first case, the guy fished out of a creek. But this one got her attention. She read the report again. Munny's vehicle was found at his apartment in its assigned parking place. She drummed her fingers on the desk.

Why two vehicles at the scene? Two hitters? No, that doesn't make sense. Did Munny drive to the meet? Then how did his truck get back to his apartment?

She moved her mug to one side and fished through the stack of file folders she kept on the left corner of her desk. Each one was labeled in green ink according to subject on the tab. She found the one labeled "Snake Shot Killer" and pulled it out.

She licked her thumb and opened the folder, setting aside the area maps she'd printed a few days earlier. Printouts of newspaper articles went in another stack until she found the single piece of paper with dates down the left-hand side. She made a note to check with the DEA liaison agent—she rolled her eyes at that fictitious title—when he came in.

HACK

He chose one of his blue suits. Not that the color—or even the fact that it was a suit—mattered in these parts, he mused as he finished the Windsor knot at his throat. But a profession, regardless of the legality or morality of that profession, required a certain code. Even if these rednecks didn't appreciate it. He smiled at his reflection in the bathroom mirror. He knew he had to include himself in the similar category of "hillbilly." But he also chose to consider himself enlightened. Transformed.

The cities he hated had played a large part in his transformation. In the cities, you could either disappear or become a beacon—or both. He discovered this curious duality in Cincinnati the hard way—two years in an Ohio penitentiary hard—and honed it in Lexington and Nashville until it became a part of his methodology: first a beacon, then a ghost. He practiced it like a musician until he mastered it, knew every note and chord, every tempo and key change as if he had been born with it. His performances had been flawless, with the single exception of Knoxville. He frowned at the mirror. A single exception, a misjudgment of the girl's resiliency. A matter, he reminded himself, that could—should—have vanished like wood smoke on an evening breeze were it not for the incompetence of the men assigned to him. Men he had not requested or selected.

He put the thought aside. He would not make that mistake again. Since that incident, he had been even more meticulous about selection. And more wary.

Today, he would be a beacon. He took his jacket from the closet and inspected it.

He had one man, Dee, working for him, a man he had selected himself after careful due diligence. Dee was greedy and not very bright, but he was steady.

His phone pinged from the bed. He stared at the glowing screen, bemused by the unexpected noise. The caller ID read "Brinks."

"Yes, Mr. Brinks," he said as he punched the button. He listened as Brad Brinks told him of his wife's arrest, his admonitions to her to keep her big mouth shut, and his assurance that Cheryl had said nothing to Sheriff Harper.

"And I suppose I am to simply take you at your word on this?" he said when Brinks finished speaking.

Silence. Then, "Mr. Hack, I swear 'fore God, she didn't say a goddamn thing. I'd'a knowed it if she did."

"Well, if she did, I will soon know," he said. "And our next conversation will most assuredly not be as pleasant as this one."

"Yes, sir. I understand. Uh…"

"Yes?"

"You got all the information you need from us?"

"That's not your concern."

"I 'pologize," Brinks said.

"You thought that if I had, you and the missus would be off the hook, is that it?"

Brinks sighed. Hack could imagine the cringing man at the other end. "Something like that. I mean, we done what you asked and found out where he lives and who he associates with and all that."

He pulled his jacket on, let Brinks sweat for another moment. "Mr. Brinks," he said as he stepped toward the door, "I'm done with you and your drunken wife when I say I'm done. Is that clear?"

"Yessir."

"In the meantime, you will be at my disposal and do exactly what I say, or you and your wife will disappear from the face of the earth as if you never existed."

"Yessir."

He punched off the call.

Twenty minutes later, he slid into the booth Dee had chosen at the highway café not far from Aberdeen, a tiny town about a half hour north of Lowndes County, near the Tombigbee River. He fought to contain a grimace as his trousers slid across the cheap vinyl bench seat. Dee sipped coffee from a mug and wore a mask of nonchalance. The menu sat unopened on the table between them. Before he could speak, a skinny waitress appeared with a pot and another mug. He nodded, and she filled the mug, topped off Dee's and said she'd be back when they'd had a minute to look at the menu. He nodded again. She spun, her sneakers squeaking on the vinyl floor, and retreated to the kitchen.

Dee surveyed him from across the top of his mug. "Nice suit," he said.

He stared back at Dee: jeans, black hoodie, diamond earring in his left ear. He never understood the compulsion for black males to dress so stereotypically. But he never offered sartorial advice. He preferred to simply be an example, a beacon.

"What do you have on our sheriff?" he said to Dee.

Dee shrugged. "Lives out near the state line. Divorced. No girlfriend, but he was banging some stripper for a while. She took off about a year ago. He sounds like one mean cat. Shoots people 'bout like you do. One guy in a bar last year, another guy in a parking lot before that. Plus a murder suspect."

"The parking lot—that was Kenny Jenkins, one of Brooks's employees," he said.

"You say so. Dude in the bar was some local psycho redneck badass 'round town. Guy name O. W. Banks. He shot the murder suspect in both legs in the dude's apartment after his deputy— longtime buddy of his—took a bullet to the side of the head."

"Longtime buddy, you say."

Dee sipped his coffee. "Yeah, apparently they was in the Marine Corps or some shit together. Couple badass loyal dudes, you know? The deputy just showed up one day after Harper got elected. Big sumbitch from Chicago. Seems like they hardly go anywhere without covering each other's backs."

He nodded. "Anything else?"

"Yeah, his father shot himself," Dee said.

"I knew about that," he said.

Dee's eyebrows shot up.

"Brad Brinks and I had a conversation," he said. "A few days back. Never hurts to corroborate information."

Dee shrugged. "Apparently, the old man was an asshole anyway, but the story was he killed a man—a *black* man—long time ago and never did time for it. Some reporter got ahold of the story and ran it in the paper, so your sheriff was about to arrest his father for murder. Till the old man blew his own head off."

He couldn't help but shake his head. "Go on," he said as he signaled the waitress for a refill on his coffee.

"He also had a big case 'round about this time. Some kid got killed in what turned out to be a deal gone bad. Kid was the son of a friend of his, which I thought was unusual."

The waitress came and went. "How so?" he said when she was out of earshot.

"The kid—Clifford Raines—was black. As was the kid's momma. But apparently his momma and this Harper dude go way back. High school. Good friends. Rumor is maybe more than friends."

"Interesting. Do you have a name?"

Dee nodded. "Rhonda Raines. Has a job at the courthouse."

He filed away all this information, especially the item regarding the Raines woman. "Have you made contact with our person in the area?"

Dee nodded, opened the menu. "Yeah, told him what was up. He'd already heard most of it." Dee glanced at him, then back down at the menu. "The part about Pritchard and Munny getting shot."

This pleased him. His role of ghost assassin continued to make its presence felt. The waitress returned as a smile crept across his face; she mistook its source. He and Dee ordered in single syllables and were again left to themselves.

"He said people are getting pissed off and a little shaky," Dee said. "First, somebody's ripping off the dealers, then the dealers are getting shot. Everybody knows Munny got his eyeballs shot out. They think that's pretty fucked up. They the ones getting ripped off, then they get shot. They know it's some kind of punishment. But they don't know shit else. Don't know who's ripping them off and no idea who's running around shooting motherfuckers in the eyes."

The waitress returned with their plates. Dee dove into scrambled eggs and toast. He pushed his own plate aside and hooked a finger through his mug. "He say anything else?"

Dee mumbled a "yeah" and nodded. "Him and another dude meeting for a sale down near Columbus in a couple of nights."

"Good," he said. "Make arrangements to accompany them. He tried the coffee, set the mug back down.

Dee stopped chewing and stared. "What's up with that?" he asked.

"Here's what it is, Dee," he said. "You're going to tell this guy that we are going to be taking a much higher level of interest in the operation in east Mississippi. You're also going to find us a base—a quiet, run-of-the-mill house that we can operate out of. And you're going to watch these redneck dealers and see what is going on out there that gets them robbed. And you're not going to ask me a lot of questions."

Dee drained his coffee and nodded. "I'll get on it."

COLT

O ne thing about Freddie Mac Baldwin—he was efficient. Munny hadn't been dead a day and a half, and only discovered sixteen hours ago, and he was reading the coroner's report.

He skimmed the part about cause of death—it was pretty obvious to him what brought about Rick Munny's demise—and noted the body had been lying in the woods less than a day, time of death about twenty-four hours prior to discovery. That put Munny shot where he was found day before yesterday.

The personal effects sheet had what he was looking for: the list of personal effects did not list car keys. In fact, there was no listing of any kind of keys. ID, wallet, cigarette lighter, small tactical knife, loose change.

"John," he called from his desk.

When John stuck his head in the door, he picked up the report. "You got the Pritchard report handy?"

John nodded, disappeared, and returned in less than a minute with the manila folder.

He took the folder and flipped through the pages. "Pritchard's personal effects don't include keys, either," he said.

John shrugged.

He shook his head. "Two sets of tracks at the Munny scene. Why?"

John pulled a chair to the desk and sat. "I see," he said. "One would presume Munny would have gotten there under his own power."

"Right. And if he didn't, why were there two vehicles there? Do me a favor. Check his DMV record, check his vehicle, then his residence."

"You think somebody drove his car away from the scene?"

He leaned back in his chair. "Possible. But it would mean more than one person involved." He had an idea. "See if you can do the same with Pritchard."

John rose, and he handed him the reports. "I'm going to see Burton and see what he knows. Call me when you get something."

"Will do," John said. He lingered over the desk.

"You got something else?"

John looked nervous as a cat. "Can I ask you something?" he said.

"Sure."

"You and Rhonda. Were y'all ever a, you know, thing?"

He jerked his head up. "A *thing?*"

John put his hands up. "Hey, man, I don't mean nothing. We been square on this ever since me and Rhonda started dating. But it's just, you know, y'all obviously been friends forever, and I know y'all are close."

He glared at John. "No," he said slowly. "We were not a thing. You're right, we're close. Always have been. So don't make me come after you, ahite?" He grinned, hoping it would change the subject.

John stepped back. Finally, a smile crept across his face. "Yeah, man, I hear you. OK." He turned and left the office.

He pulled out his cell and texted Burton, checked his watch, and then headed out to his car.

Fifteen minutes later, he killed the engine and cut off his headlights in a Mexican restaurant parking lot just off Highway 45, near the back entrance, then texted Burton, who was inside, if the presence of his car in the lot was any indication.

Burton rounded the darkened corner of the building about two minutes later, green neon light reflecting off his John Lennon glasses, making him look like some kind of hippie alien.

He slid out of the car and quick-stepped to catch Burton near the side of the building, up against the white-painted brick wall. Burton jumped, not expecting the onrush, as he grabbed him by the shoulders and shoved him against the wall.

"Shit, Sheriff, what's going on?" Burton asked, eyes wide behind the lenses.

"I ask the questions in this relationship, Jimbo, and you provide the answers," he said, his face inches from Burton's. "That's what an informant does. He informs. You, on the other hand, ain't told me shit."

Burton tried to wriggle free, so he shoved the hippie alien harder, pinning him to the wall.

"The fuck, Harper?"

"I asked you if you knew anything dealers getting ripped off, and you told me a lie."

"I did not."

"Oh, so it's just a coincidence that your name is in a report with two other dope dealers, both of whom are now dead."

Burton froze, terrified. "Whoa, whoa, slow down. What the hell you talking about?"

"I pulled Robert Pritchard out of the Lux a few days ago. Turns out he had a record. And his list of known associates includes your sorry ass and another dealer named Rick Munny."

Burton chewed his lip. "Are you shitting me? Robert Pritchard is dead?"

"Shot and dumped in the creek."

"And Munny, too?"

"He had his eyes shot out. So you better start talking or I'm going to decide that the tequila I'm smelling all over you constitutes a parole violation."

He released his grip and stepped back to show Burton he was being reasonable. Burton made a big show of rubbing his shoulders and looking indignant.

"Look, Harper," he said, "I'd heard that Munny and Pritchard got ripped off. That's all. I don't know nothing about them getting shot."

He shoved Burton back against the wall, grabbing him by the throat. "Nothing, huh? What else do you know nothing about?"

Burton was back to wriggling like a snake caught by its head. He put both hands up in surrender. "Shit, man, that's all I know. Pritchard ran oxy for McNairy. They did most of their business out of Winnie's.

"Winnie's? That old broken-down shit bar in town? East side?"

"That's the one."

He caught Burton's roving, wild eyes and locked onto them with his own. "What else?"

"Ain't nothing else. That's all I know. Rest is people talking shit, you know?"

"Yeah?" He let go of Burton's throat.

"Thank you," Burton said with as much sarcasm as he dared. "That shit hurts, you know."

"It's supposed to, dumbass."

Burton pushed his stringy hair out of his face.

He nodded. "Ahite, get the fuck out of here. And if you hear something, don't make me come after you again."

Burton took a step to the side, toward the front of the building. "OK, OK," he said.

He left Burton standing next to the wall, shaking, climbed into the Crown Vic, and roared onto the highway without a glance back.

DELMER

He couldn't decide who was dumber, the drug users or the drug dealers.

Both were pretty fucking stupid. The crankheads were stupid for paying what they did to get high. The dealers, on the other hand, didn't seem to know shit about low profile. Easiest way to find a drug dealer in east Mississippi was to look for the redneck with the most tricked-out pickup or muscle car. You could damn near bet on it being a dealer.

He sat in his Mazda, tucked up against the side of a nail salon in what passed for downtown Caledonia, and peered through the windshield at the Dodge parked across the street. He was confident he couldn't be seen. The Mazda was small and a good six feet outside the yellow areola of the streetlight on the curb. To his right, a massive oak darkened the gravel alleyway.

He'd been watching the brand-new Charger for twenty minutes, since it pulled up and came to a stop in the darkened empty lot next to a drive-through pharmacy that sat catty-corner from his vantage point, at a downtown intersection. Nobody had gotten out of the car, or turned on a dome light, and nobody had approached the car. That meant the deal was still on. Would be until the Dodge left. All he had to do was wait. And when the crankhead showed, he'd close the forty feet separating his car from the dealer before anyone could react, rob them both, and be on his way. He had the .44 and the zombie mask sitting on the passenger seat beside him. Too hot to pull that mask on until he absolutely had to. So he waited.

Looking back at the Munny job now, that one had been a rookie move, like the first one. Home invasions were stupid, even if most dealers got robbed that way. Only one way in and out. And you don't know the lay of the land, so to speak. So he refined his approach. Tonight he had maneuver room. And what the military manuals he'd read as a kid called "avenues of approach."

He caught a glint of light in his peripheral vision, off to the left. He scooted lower behind the wheel and watched a Honda creep down the street, then pull up alongside the Dodge.

Game on.

He popped the door handle and waited. The Honda went silent, lights out, and the driver emerged. White guy, jeans, baseball jersey of some kind, ball cap. The dude swiveled his head left and right, then scurried around the hood to the Charger.

He peered at the Honda's passenger seat. Looked empty. He eased his door open, stepped out, and clicked it shut. He put his back against the wall of the store, pulled the mask over his head, and stuck the pistol in the back of his jeans. He peeked around the corner of the building for traffic, saw none in either direction, and quick-stepped across the street, avoiding the streetlight as he went.

He came up on the right rear quarter panel of the Dodge in what he hoped was the driver's blind spot. He heard the buyer say, "Yeah, two-fifty" as he stepped between the two cars and drew his pistol.

"OK, asshole, right there," he said.

The buyer jumped straight up and back. "What the fuck, man? Who the fuck are you?"

Delmer adjusted his aim slightly. "In the car. Hands out the window. Both of them." He couldn't see the driver or inside the car. He thumbcocked the revolver, more for effect than anything. It worked. The loud metallic *click-click* caused two hands to emerge from the window. White hands belonging to a man. So far, so good.

"You," he said, returning his attention to the crankhead standing by the car. "Hit your knees. Hands behind your head."

He stepped to the driver's window, leaned over to eyeball the driver, a twenty-something guy with a nasty beard who looked as terrified as the buyer. He put the gun against the driver's temple.

"You," he said, "are going to hand over whatever cash you got in there. And if you even think about reaching for a piece, I'm going to trade you and your cash for one of my bullets. Understand?"

The driver nodded. "Yeah, man, I understand. You're crazy as hell, but I understand. I got to pull my hands back in the car, though."

"Where's the money?"

"Glove compartment."

"Do it."

The driver reached over, popped the compartment open, and reached inside. Delmer reminded him of the gun against his head by nudging him with the muzzle. The driver pulled out a stack of bills, held together with rubber bands on each end, and leaned back behind the wheel. He held it up. "Here it is."

Delmer took the money and stuffed in his back pocket. "See how easy that was? Cell phones."

"What?" the driver said.

"Cell phones. Both of you. Right now."

The driver sighed, picked up the phone off the seat, and handed it over. Delmer took it, hurled it over the top of the car, and heard it smack against something hard.

"That didn't sound good," he said.

"Asshole."

He turned to the buyer. "One hand."

The buyer's head bobbed up and down. He reached into a pocket and produced his phone. Delmer flung it over his head into the darkness behind the pharmacy building. It smacked the concrete with a crunch.

"Now, you're both going to sit right where you are for the next ten minutes and not say a word. And if you do, I'll know, and I'll be back, hear?"

The buyer nodded. The driver exhaled loudly. "Yeah," he said. "I hear you. You are one dumb sumbitch."

"Yeah?" Delmer said. "Well, I'm the one with the gun and the money."

He backed away from the cars, the gun still trained on the buyer. When he reached the street, he turned and trotted back to his car tucked away in the darkness. He jumped in, cranked up, and backed away from the scene and around the back of the nail salon. Certain he couldn't be seen by his victims, he pulled out onto a darkened street and headed out of town. He'd count the money once he made the highway.

COLT

He dropped the phone back into the cradle on his desk and yelled for John.

"What's up, Colt?" John said when he poked his head through the door.

"Saddle up," he said. "I need you to go with me."

John nodded. "Let's roll, then."

They didn't speak on the short walk to the car. John never asked questions because he didn't need to, especially in a situation like this. They'd rolled into situations plenty of times out at Camp Pendleton when they'd been temporarily assigned to the MP battalion.

"I just got off the phone with Burton," he said as he wheeled out of the lot. "Said there was another dope deal ripoff couple of nights ago, right in the middle of downtown Caledonia."

John shook his head. "Again? We got some kind of crime spree going on, looks like."

"Looks like," he said. "Burton said one of the guys got ripped off hangs out at Winnie's, same place Pritchard ran oxy out of for those idiots up in McNairy County."

"And you trust Burton on this?" John asked.

He cut his eyes at John. "Look, Burton's dumber'n a hammer, but he's smart enough to not bullshit me when he knows I'm about to run his ass on a parole violation."

John laughed. "Fair enough. So I take it we're headed to this Winnie's joint?"

"Yeah." He stopped a red light. "I'm going to need you as backup only on this. Outside. Just cover all the doors. Ain't but two."

Now John turned to look at him. "Outside? Why outside?"

He kept his face neutral and stared ahead through the windshield. "This place ain't exactly what you'd call a diverse environment. It's going to be bad enough me walking in there. Don't need to make it worse."

John shook his head. "Fuck that." He sighed. "Sometimes, man…"

"I know. But this is the kind of place where you drink beer out of a bottle so you always got a weapon in your hand—know what I mean? And a man of your…height might not be very welcome there."

John nodded. He could tell John was pissed, but pissed was better than being shot. Again. Last thing he needed was Rhonda on his ass for getting John hurt.

"Here we are." He threw the car up in park and checked the lot. Not a single light, with cars and more than a few pickup trucks parked haphazardly over a patch of asphalt that looked like it had been bombed, repaved, and bombed again.

Winnie's was the same on the outside as it was since he first walked into the joint as a teenager on a dare. A low metal building, unmarked and unremarkable except for a small white sign by the door that read, *"Winnie's. 21 and up."*

"Take the shotgun," he said to John and pointed to a side door. "And watch these doors."

John was out the door and racking a shell into the shotgun's chamber before he could round the back of the car.

He stepped into the sweltering, dim hole of a bar and noticed the thick smoke had a whiff of weed to it. A pool table with stained felt and a stack of quarters on one rail dominated the concrete floor, and a bar built out of old wooden crates took up the entire back wall. The whole place reeked of sweat, beer, puke, and smoke. *Some things never change*, he thought as he eyed two pool players staring back at him. Behind them, a group of four men shifted their feet as they recognized that The Law had just stepped in to ruin their Saturday night.

He walked to the table and picked up the cue ball, tossed it from one hand to the other. One of the players, tall guy with a beard and hard eyes, sighed and leaned his stick against the wall.

"Evening, fellas," he said. "Hate to interrupt the game and all, but business is business."

One of the back group moved his way to the front. "We ain't doin' nothin', Harper," he said.

He put the cue ball in his pocket. "Well, Pete Harris, how the hell are you?" he said, grinning. "Haven't seen you around in a while. How's those anger management courses going? Court-ordered, right?"

Harris rolled his eyes. Took a pull on his beer. "Yeah, right," he said.

"Excuse me, Pete, I'd love to discuss those classes and what you've learned and how it's going to help your marriage, but we're going to have to catch up later," he said. "Now, I just got a couple of questions for y'all, and if y'all cooperate and act right, I'll be out of your hair in no time. If y'all want to act up, we might be here all night after I shut this place down."

The tall pool player crossed his arms. "This is bullshit, Sheriff. We ain't doing nothing but shooting pool, and you ain't got no warrant."

He stared at the man. "Warrant? You kidding me? I don't need a warrant to stop off on my way home for a beer and game of pool."

"Like I said, we ain't doing nothing."

"You know what me and a dead owl got in common? Neither one of us give a hoot. What I do give a hoot about is the dope dealers getting ripped off in this county all of a sudden. To be a little bit more specific, the person ripping off these dealers and then killing them. Word is, Robert Pritchard ran his oxy out of here up until he got killed. And so did a dealer who got ripped off a couple of nights ago over in Caledonia. Not to mention poor ol' Rick Munny, who got his eyes shot out over in Bishop's Bottom."

The bartender, a bald man in a black T-shirt with several bad tattoos, started to make his way around the bar.

He put his hand on his holster. "You just stay right there."

The bartender, who looked about as rough as his customers, stopped and glared at him. "You can't just come in here and accuse me of that kind of shit, Sheriff."

He looked around the room. "Boy, y'all seem to know a lot about the law. Anyway, somebody else got ripped off the other night, by a man wearing some kind of Halloween mask, a zombie or some shit. Same guy, I'm guessing, who killed Pritchard and Munny. Made off with a few thousand dollars like it was nothing. And the dealer who got ripped off was last seen here, drinking and playing pool. Now, y'all are a bunch of pool players, drinkers, and otherwise general degenerates, and the question is, any of you know anything about this?"

Shoes shuffled on the dirty concrete and a couple of men coughed. He stared at each in turn. One, a short, young guy with blond hair and rat eyes, avoided his gaze, then yanked open the side door and bolted into the blackness outside. The others jumped at the sound of the door slamming shut behind him.

He looked at the group, shook his head. "Really, guys? Nothing? Ahite, then." He pulled out his cell phone. "Great things these smart phones. I can get y'all's pictures and just run them when I get back to the office." He stared clicking mug shots as the men put on hostile faces and tried to ignore him.

The side door burst open with a rusty-hinge scream and the rat-eyed boy tumbled back in, bent over at the waist with John's big hand on the scruff of his neck, shotgun in his other hand.

"Well, that didn't take long, John," he said, noticing the group was suddenly interested in everything he had to say.

"Everything OK in here?" John said. The muscles in his forearm flexed as he forced the kid upright.

He nodded and pocketed his phone. "Just fine, John. Just fine. Me and the boys here were just finishing up our photo session."

John grinned. "I should probably introduce you to this one."

"Good idea," he said. "I'll meet you at the car."

"Roger." John snatched the kid around and shoved him out the side door.

"Fellas, y'all got lucky tonight," he said. "But I do appreciate the photos. I'm sure there's a couple of parole officers who are going to be interested in them. So any of y'all hear anything, know anything, you think about that, y'hear?"

He turned and walked outside, where John had the kid bent over the trunk of the Crown Vic, handcuffed and terrified, but otherwise in good shape.

John cocked his head toward the kid. "Russell Quinn. Twenty. He's got about ten dollars in cash on him, driver's license. And this." He held up a tiny plastic bag.

He shook his head. "Russell, this ain't your lucky day, is it?"

"That shit ain't mine," Quinn said, his cheek still against the car."

"Right," he said. "Eight ball just fell into your pocket." He leaned against the car and looked at Quinn's squinting eyes. "Now, look, Russell, here's what I think. I'm going to bet you got a bunch of priors—possession, theft, B and E, that kind of thing. You on probation?"

Quinn nodded. "Yeah."

"Yeah. But you didn't bolt as soon as I walked into the place, which would have been the smart thing to do. I mean, the law shows up, you haul ass. That's Rule Number One in Dopehead World. But you didn't. You took off when I mentioned the rip-off last night. So I think you know something. And I'm going to go out on a limb here and say you'd just as soon not go to jail, nice blond white boy like yourself. Am I right?"

He squinted and nodded. "Yes, damn it. But I didn't have anything to do with that shit that went down last night."

"Naw, I don't figure you did," he said. "But you know something. So start talking."

Quinn sighed. "I was here late last night. I'd already scored that eight-ball, and I was here drinking and hanging out. About ten or eleven, I saw a guy come in, looking like he was looking for somebody. He ordered a beer and hung at the bar for about twenty minutes. Then it didn't look like he found who he was looking for, so he left."

He looked at John, who nodded at him. "You got a name?" he said to Quinn.

"I don't know the guy at all, but his name's Blackburn. Delmer Blackburn. I seen him in there a few times."

He pulled Quinn upright and turned him around so that he was facing him. "A few times? Same as this time?"

Quinn nodded. "Pretty much. He shows up, does some drinking, then takes off."

"Always alone?"

"Yeah, except one time, I thought he was talking to that dealer name of Pritchard, but he was just drinking beside him."

"You sure of that? That it was Pritchard?"

"Hell yeah," Quinn said. "I was trying to buy something off Pritchard that night."

"All right, Russell," he said. Then to John, "Take the cuffs off."

John stepped over and grabbed Quinn by his cuffs. "What about the dope?"

He looked at Russell. "Get the fuck out of here. And if I run across you again, I'm going to throw your ass in jail for possession of meth."

Quinn rubbed his wrists and without a word, turned and fled, disappearing across the street and into a vacant darkened lot.

He looked at John. "Put that shit in the safe in my office. In case we need it for young Russell there."

MOLLY

She put her hands on her hips and exhaled. The living room floor of her apartment was littered with reports, crime scene photos, autopsy photos, case files, her own notes, and maps of Mississippi and Alabama torn from a road atlas then taped together.

The living room looked as if someone had dumped the contents of a file cabinet in the middle the floor. But, as she stood in pajama bottoms and a Virginia Tech T-shirt, she knew where every piece was and its relationship to every other piece. "Organized chaos," she called it. She could have done it all on her laptop, but she was a tactile person, and preferred the feel of the paper in her hands when she had a hunch.

She glanced at her watch: 0241. She was nearly done. She had spent the last seven hours organizing the piles, writing, and amending her notes.

She squatted, and her hands flew like a concert pianist's over the various files and folders, stacking piles in alternate fashion—portrait, landscape, portrait, landscape, and so on. She hoisted the resulting stack, nearly a foot tall, and set it with the rough care of a brick mason on the coffee table.

She needed sleep. She had reserved the conference room for herself at 0800, so that she could avail herself of the whiteboard that took up nearly the entire wall on one side.

She sat on the couch, staring at the stack of files that represented two weeks of her work—on her own time—and refreshing her thought process. She was aware that she was taking a long shot and working off hunches—maybe too many hunches—on a case that wasn't really a case, and one to which she had not been assigned even if it were.

The snake shot wouldn't leave her alone. Ever since she'd overheard the conversation in the break room, it nagged her. And when the second body was discovered—the one with his eyes shot out—she knew it wasn't a coincidence. She'd listened around the office, read reports, even chatted up a DEA guy she knew, but nobody seemed to connect the dots. She kept it to herself and started digging.

She had shaken down her admittedly short list of contacts, both in ATF and her network of informants and gossips. The only thing she learned was that, in east Mississippi, somebody rumored to be an enforcer for a boss in Memphis was punishing dealers who had been robbed by a person or persons unknown. But that was based on nothing but the hearsay of snitches and dopeheads.

She started with the reports on the first victim, Robert Pritchard. She studied terrain and road maps of the area where the body was found. The report did not state definitively if the murder occurred on the bank or if the body was transported there and dumped. Hunch Number One: Pritchard was shot upstream and floated down.

She researched the conditions and hydrography of the Luxapalila Creek and its currents to get an idea of how far the body would have traveled, using a best- and worst-case scenario. That gave her two circles—one about thirty miles, the other about fifty—upstream from the place of discovery. That was a lot of territory. To find something she wasn't even able to identify yet.

She'd spent an afternoon going through the coroner's report and asking questions of a retired medical examiner she consulted on occasion, a serious woman named Beatrice Patterson. Patterson shot holes in her hypothesis, which was good. She had learned a long time ago that professionals critique to help as well help to critique.

"Unless the body had something attached to it from upstream or was marked in some way—say, gashed from what would be a bridge piling, something like that—it's really hard to say exactly how or where the body got into the water," Patterson said. "You read the report and saw the photos. Except for the GSW, it would almost look like a drowning."

Patterson recommended she not put too much stock into charting river currents, either. Unlike herself, Patterson was a local and had grown up along a river. She knew a river's moods and peculiarities the way long-married couples know their spouses.

"Unless you knew the exact weather conditions at the time of death, which is itself an approximation," Patterson told her, "and the exact flow data of the river on that particular day, you're really just making wild-ass guesses."

But after she'd gotten back to her apartment, she remembered Patterson had mentioned a bridge. As an example, sure, but it gave her an idea. On the map, she circled every bridge upstream from the scene for sixty miles. The location of Pritchard's body was marked on the map with a square and the number one in it. She reread the list of his personal effects collected by the morgue team and, sure enough, his car keys were listed. There was no notation of make and model, which probably meant no one had bothered to run down the car. That went into her notes for later, but, playing a hunch, she started at the bridges closest to the scene. Several spanned the creek in or near Columbus, and she quickly discounted those. That left three others farther upstream, one of which actually traversed a smaller creek that fed into the river.

Google Earth showed all three were in rural areas. The bridge over the small creek most of all. It was possible that Pritchard had been dumped from one of those bridges and maybe even killed there. Those bridges were on her list and in her PowerPoint presentation—while she loved the old-fashioned way, tomorrow morning's brief—this morning, she corrected herself—would be modern.

The second victim, Rick Munny, had been found on a dirt road deep in a wooded area in a rural part of the county. Munny was also killed with snake shot. But, unlike Pritchard, his keys were not among his personal effects. His truck was parked in front of his residence when time of death occurred. No sign of a struggle. A very deliberate murder. Munny's location was a square on the map with the number two written inside.

She closed her eyes and lay back on the couch and willed sleep to come, but it wouldn't. One thought kept pouncing through her mind: *I really need this. For seven fucking years, I've needed this.*

She hoped to change that at 0800. As her eyelids at last drooped, she was aware of the desperation in her hope.

DELMER

"And you're sure about that?" he asked Ray for the fourth time.

They sat on the hood of his car in a small parking lot overlooking the lock and dam. He and Ray had gone to school together, but the only time they ever saw each other these days was at Winnie's. He'd watched Ray sidle up to a guy he knew to be a dealer, dude named Turn, the other night as if he was trying to score.

He'd followed Ray and Turn out to the parking lot of the bar and watched the deal go down from the shadows of the building.

So for the last couple of days he'd been real friendly with Ray, playing the part of another dopehead looking to score some oxy.

Once Ray agreed to arrange a deal with Turn, he began his routine of getting the info on Turn, especially the part about a gun. Turn had a rep as a badass.

"Man, why do you keep asking that?" Ray said. "I done told you he don't carry a gun."

"Just making sure."

Ray shook his head and slid off the hood. Tossed his empty beer bottle into the tall grass on the slope that led down to the dam. "He's scary enough to not need one."

"Yeah, that's true," he said. "So Turn is big business, huh?"

Ray pulled another longneck from the six-pack sitting on the pavement in front of the car, twisted it open. "Yeah, he deals a lot around here and always has cash on him."

He sat up, but tried not to look too interested.

"Yeah? How much is a lot?"

Ray looked at him, and he saw a lot of anxiety in the man's eyes. Ray had the look of a man scared to tell a secret but dying not to.

"Word is," Ray said, "he's got a rolling bank in his car. Keeps about fifty grand in it."

He drained his own beer. "Bullshit. Fifty grand? No way."

Ray shrugged. "That's the word going around. I seen him with a big wad of cash every time I run into him. I know that."

"Damn, dude with that much cash ought to be careful."

Ray's head bobbed as he stared at the glassy surface of the Tombigbee below them. "So, we on, then?" he said. "Tomorrow night?"

He slid off the car, picked up the remaining longnecks. "Definitely," he said. "I'll be there."

"Cool. "I'll let Turn know."

COLT

John walked in and stood in front of his desk, waited for him to finish reading the Munny report. He closed the folder, looked up.

"What you got?"

John grabbed the chair by the desk, pulled it to him, and sat. "Not much on Delmer Blackburn. But what's bugging you?"

He leaned back in his chair. "We noticed it at the scene. Two sets of tracks, two different vehicles. I just read the report on Munny, including the girlfriend's statement. Munny's truck was found parked at his apartment after we found him dead. She said he'd left sometime the night before in his vehicle, and she never heard him come home. Had no idea where he'd planned to go that night, and she was with some other guy until midnight. But, yet, his truck was there the next morning—the morning after we found him dead. And no keys in Munny's personal effects."

"Girlfriend got a set?" John asked.

He shook his head. "She said she didn't. And if she doesn't and none were found on Munny, that means somebody probably drove his vehicle away from the scene and somebody else drove the other vehicle."

John nodded. "And we haven't heard anything about two people being involved. You think this Blackburn has a crew?"

He shrugged. "I have no idea. But it looks like somebody does. What you got on Blackburn?"

"Like I said, nothing much. No priors. Speeding ticket two years ago."

"That's it?"

John nodded. "I know. Doesn't give us much to go on."

"No shit," he said. "Can't arrest a man for being invisible."

"We can ask him to come in for questioning, though."

"That's what I'm thinking," he said. "Got an address?"

"Sure."

"Go bring his ass in, then, and let's see what he has to say."

DELMER

He had never shot anyone until about thirty seconds ago.

He thumbcocked the Magnum and pointed it at the corpse lying facedown in the gravel behind the Monte Carlo. The glow of the taillights illuminated the growing pool of blood, casting it black as oil in the dim light.

Turn was dead, had to be. The hollow-point bullet from the .44 had hit him square in the chest at near point-blank range.

He had never even fired a gun at a man before, and now two lay dead at his feet. Behind him, near the driver's side door, Ray lay sprawled on the warm blacktop, surely dead, eyes glaring at the night sky above, a bullet hole in his right cheek and a pattern of blood, brain, and bone sprayed across the southbound lane of Highway 12.

Turn's feet twitched, and he thought about putting another one in him, but then Turn went still, so he eased the hammer down.

This shit did not go down the way I wanted it to.

He stared at the black wall of trees across the highway, then at the blood trail that led from Ray's side, across the asphalt, into the gravel and the ditch on the other side.

The third guy ran off into those woods. But he was hit pretty good, judging from the blotches of blood.

His heart felt like it was trying to strangle him, and his hands shook. He gripped the pistol and stared, his mind flinging words that weren't even coherent thoughts around in his head.

He needed to calm down, make this shit make sense, but all he could do was stare at the woods. Which was stupid if the guy he shot had a gun. Which he most assuredly did.

Who the fuck was that guy?

It wasn't supposed to go like this. Hell, he considered Ray to be something close to a friend. Not drinking buddies or anything, but someone he'd known most of his life. He surely wouldn't have bet he'd be blowing a hole in him tonight.

What the fuck just happened?

He finally gathered his wits and ran to the driver's side of Ray's car, reached into the backseat and grabbed the gym bag back there. He opened it on the trunk, rummaged through the contents. Pill bottles clattered in the bottom. A speedloader. Baggie of weed, which he pocketed. No money.

"Fuck!" he yelled into the bag. "There has to be fucking money."

He spun around and looked at Ray. The money had to still be on him. He swallowed bile. No way he wanted to touch the man he'd just killed. He huffed out a breath, shook his head, and squatted over Ray. Patted him down, still nothing.

"Shit, of course this ain't going to be easy. Thanks a lot, Ray."

He rolled the body over and saw the envelope sticking from the pocket of the jeans. He grabbed it and sprinted to his car. He really didn't give a shit how much was in the envelope, and he could tell by feel that it wasn't much—not nearly what he'd expected. But he damn sure wasn't going to leave that scene empty-handed. Not after that.

He put the car in gear and flew down the highway headed north, away from town. Away from everything. He had to think. Something had felt wrong from the minute Ray got out of his car.

He'd set the deal with Ray three days ago. Ray didn't do any dealing, but he knew the guy who did. Turn—Kevin Turner—had been running oxy for a while, and Ray was a regular customer. They'd bumped into each other over a beer at Winnie's, and one thing led to another. He let on that he might be looking to score, and Ray was obliging.

He'd even pressed Ray for a little intel—did Turn carry a gun or money, that kind of thing. Ray said he'd never seen him with a gun, and the only money he knew about was the cash he handed over for his dope.

Well, he sure as shit had a gun tonight. And so did Ray, that little shit.

They'd met at a rest stop that been closed down years ago, right off the highway. He'd pulled up behind them and gotten out, the .44 in the back of his pants. Ray climbed out of the driver's side, looking nervous as hell. He picked up on that right away—Ray looked like he wanted to be anywhere in the world but on the side of Highway 12 at that moment. Then Turn climbed out of the passenger side with an auto in his hand. At the same time, a black kid he'd never seen damn near jumped out of the backseat on Ray's side, also holding a pistol.

He'd decided to play it cool and took on a look of confusion.

"Hey, Ray, what's up with all the guns?"

Ray just shook his head, and for the first time he noticed the gun in Ray's right hand. He was holding it down at his side, almost like he was embarrassed to be carrying it. Or didn't want to.

It was Turn who spoke. "Precautions. Or comeuppance, take your pick," he said.

He shrugged. "I don't know what you mean."

Turn was big man, over six feet, with a full beard and hair that fell to his shoulders like a woman's. He took a step toward Delmer and looked a lot taller. "You the little fucker been ripping dealers off."

His bowels cramped, and his throat seized up. He glared back at Turn and tried to keep an eye on the black kid, who had moved around the car and to Turn's left about three feet. "What?" he yelled, hoping he sounded sufficiently shocked.

Turn snickered. "Folks saw you at Winnie's the night Pritchard got robbed. And you set up this deal at Winnie's with Ray over there."

Ray flinched at the sound of his name and looked guilty as shit as he took on a hurt look, then cast his eyes to the ground.

His reflexes kicked into gear. He snatched the Magnum out and started cranking off shots. One hit Turn square in the chest just as he raised and fired his own pistol. He fired twice more at the black kid in the dark, heard him howl and go down. He pivoted toward Ray, who was raising his pistol. He was so stunned at Ray's movements, he nearly forgot the consequences of Ray's actions, but he fired first. A bullet hit Ray in the face, and he flew backward and landed on the highway asphalt in a wet thud.

He spun back toward the black kid with two bullets left. Nothing. The kid was gone. At first he thought he'd missed him, then he saw the blood trail. Several splotches the size of a saucer leading through the gravel shoulder into the ditch off to the right-hand side of the road. Beyond, black woods made any surveillance impossible.

"Now what?" he said to the windshield. He punched the steering wheel. "Now fucking what?"

DEE

Dee sat with his back against a pine tree and clutched his calf with both hands. Sweat rolled off his face like rainwater.

He was afraid to move his hands, or even look at his leg, for fear of blood gushing out of his body. He didn't know how much blood he had lost, *but goddamn it hurt so probably a lot serves me right for getting involved in this cracker redneck crazy-ass shit in the first place how much blood is even in my body that shit went down way too fast and way too stupid goddamn Turn is an idiot—was an idiot—I shoulda knowed better when I laid eyes on him but Hack said he was cool. Cool my ass this is just some more Mr. Freeze bullshit and that motherfucker is definitely going pay me hell give me a raise if I ever walk again I wonder if my leg still works I can't even feel it shit it hurts that stupid white boy with his bigass Magnum I'da shot his ass dead what was his name Delmer Blackburn that's right I'da shot his ass dead if that stupid bitch Turn had any idea what he was doing amateur ass motherfucker getting out the car like he's Dirty Harry or some shit all cool after I told his dumb ass to come out the car with the gun and leveled at that punkass bitch but no he had to do it his way and that motherfucker is dead and it serves him right fuck my leg hurts I gotta get to that car and get the hell outta here before the cops show up and they will show up you know that so get on up and ease yo' ass over to that car and vanish.*

He calmed his ragged breath enough to clear his head. Ray's car still sat on the shoulder, headlights streaming into the hot

Mississippi night, two corpses cooling nearby. He yanked off a sneaker and a sock and tied the sock around the bullet wound in his right leg, still cursing Delmer's .44 Magnum. Satisfied he had stopped the blood for the moment, he put his shoe back on and pushed himself to his feet. Pain hit him behind the eyeballs, white hot, and he sagged against the tree. He took a deep breath and pushed off, stumbled up the shoulder to the car. He stepped over Turn and hobbled to the driver's side. Keys still in the ignition. Amateurs, both of them. He sagged against the driver's side.

Tonight was a first-class fuckup, no doubt, but now he had a name and a solid description for Hack. Delmer Blackburn.

"And Mr. Delmer Blackburn, very soon it's gone be yo' ass."

He hated the very thought of his next move, but he had no choice. He sure as shit wasn't going to drive off in this car and have every cop in the state looking for him. He grimaced, pulled out his phone, and punched Hack's number.

"Yes?" Hack answered.

He sighed. "Hack you ain't going to believe this one."

COLT

"**G**oddammit."

He put his hands on his hips and stared at the gory tableau on the gray, early morning highway in front of him: Monte Carlo with a faded blue paint job, both doors open, sitting in the gravel under a line of pines at a closed-down rest stop. Body on each side, both on their backs with gunshot wounds. Both male.

John walked up beside him after radioing their location. "This may explain why Blackburn wasn't home earlier."

He snorted. "Yeah, maybe." He walked to the driver's side. The dead man there wore a look of shock in his wide-open eyes and a pulpy, wet bullet hole in his cheek. Looked like most of his brain was scattered behind him on the asphalt. Cheap nickel-plated auto in his right hand. No brass nearby, so it was probably unlikely he fired the weapon.

He checked the car's interior. Nothing. No dope, no money, no guns, nothing. On the other side of the car, John knelt over the other corpse.

"Whoever did this," John said over the car, "used a big-ass weapon."

He walked around the rear of the car and knelt beside John. "Yeah, same with the other guy. Probably a Magnum or a forty-five."

John nodded. "Well, this is a big dude. Looks like a roadie for a heavy metal band."

He looked behind them, down the highway. "Shooter popped them both from somewhere back there. Other guy didn't even get off a shot. Saturday night special still in his hand."

"This guy did," John said, pointing to a brass casing a couple of feet from the body. "And that Glock in his hand ain't no Saturday night special."

He stood and walked away from the vehicle. "Well, the person called it in said he heard a series of gunshots. We've already accounted for at least three," he said as he scoured the ground to the rear of the scene. He stopped.

"Hey," he called back to John. "You see this?"

"What?"

"Blood over here. Lots of it." He pulled his flashlight and aimed it toward the large splotch, a dark red stain in the gravel of the highway shoulder.

John came over and whistled when he saw it. "Yeah, somebody took one good."

He found another, then another splash of blood leading down the slope of the shoulder, across a shallow ditch, and into the woods.

"Somebody got hit and got away," he said.

"The shooter? Delmer?"

"Naw, something ain't right here," he said, staring at the dark wall of trees. "Whoever it is robbing these dealers doesn't kill them. At least that's what I think. Let's say it's the guy doing the robbing, though. If so, this went really wrong for him. He wasn't expecting this, and when it went down, he goes Wyatt Earp on these guys, bags two of 'em."

"Makes sense," John said. "But he's got a problem."

"Yeah," he said. "One guy got away. And he's liable to be spooked now. Big time. And he may show up at a hospital."

John nodded toward the coroner's vehicle making its way up the road just as the sun topped the tree line. "I think we should put out a BOLO for Delmer Blackburn," he said.

"Do it. Armed and dangerous."

HACK

He watched Dee take a deep drag off the joint as he splashed alcohol over the leg wound.

"In the old days," he said, "You'd be drinking whiskey for the pain."

Dee winced but held his leg steady. "These ain't the old days," he said. He blew a thin stream of blue smoke toward the ceiling of the house they were now renting, a bland prefab job near the Mississippi-Alabama line just off Highway 69. "And goddamn that hurts."

"Getting shot usually does." He turned to the kitchen table and surveyed the kit spread out on a towel. "You're lucky it's a through and through, so I don't have to go digging around for the bullet. All I have to do is sew you up." He grabbed a suture needle and a loop of thread, turned to face Dee.

The boy took another hit and nodded. He was holding up well, considering he had a pretty good chunk of his calf blown out, had lost a good bit of blood, and was scared shitless.

"Yeah, well, just make sure you got some oxy handy, OK?" Dee said.

He smiled and shook his head. He reached with his free hand and gave Dee the bottle. The kid shook a few out and tossed them in his mouth, washing them down with the open bottle of beer at his feet.

He went to work sewing up the leg. "Tell me," he said.

Dee nodded. "We show up at the meet, everything is cool, 'cept for that one dumbass, Turn, wanted to go all cowboy. Dunno, maybe I shouldn't'a said what the real deal was. But I said I was there to make sure everything went smooth, he was ready to rock. We get there—"

"Who was driving?"

"Ray was," Dee said, his speech slowing from the oxy high. "That Turn cat was in the passenger seat. I was in the back."

"Who got there first?"

Dee cut him a look. "We did. You think I'm an amateur?"

He didn't look up. "No, I don't. But I want to know exactly how this went down."

"We're sitting in the car about five minutes, and the car rolls up. A Mazda. Mazda3, I think. Dark color, maybe like a midnight blue." Dee looked down at his bloody leg. "You know that shit hurts. I wasn't kidding."

Hack nodded, letting the pain meds, the weed, and the alcohol do the work on Dee.

"Anyway," Dee said, "this guy gets out and starts walking toward us. Not aggressive or nothing. Just walking. Ray gets out. Then Turn busts out the car with his piece in his hand. When I saw that, I come out, too, and we got us a Mexican standoff."

Hack knotted off the sutures and wiped the leg down. "But."

Dee nodded. "Yeah, but. Turn starts mouthing off, accusing the guy of ripping dealers off, making the guy real nervous. You could see that. I started to make my way off to Turn's left, figuring I'd flank his ass or something. But before I took two steps, the guy yanks out a fucking Magnum and goes all OK Corral. He popped Turn dead in the chest. I try to get over to the side of the road in the dark, and he hit me in the leg. Then he killed Ray."

Hack looked at him. "I thought Ray and he were buddies."

Dee shrugged. "Dunno, man. Turn told Ray to carry a piece. Maybe he thought Ray was going to draw down on him."

"Was he?"

"Shit naw. Ray's scared as a motherfucker. I don't think he even got a shot off."

"Then what?"

"I got my ass into the woods. He stood there staring right at me, but he couldn't see anything in the dark. Then he rooted around in the car, cussing and yelling. Then he drove off."

Hack started collecting up his gear and walked to the sink to rinse it off. "And that's it?"

"Nope. Wyatt Earp got away tonight, but I got his plate number. More importantly, I got his name. Delmer Blackburn."

Hack turned to Dee. "Delmer Blackburn," he said.

Dee nodded.

"Write that plate number down before you get too high to remember. Then get your ass on one of the beds and pass out."

DELMER

He couldn't go home. Not right now. And he didn't like being out in the open. For all he knew, the highway patrol or the FBI or the DEA was looking for him. He surely hoped that black guy he'd shot had bled to death, but he couldn't count on that.

Admit it, boy, you're fucked, and you don't know what to do.

He crossed over into Alabama and drove through the country roads, speeding, slowing, making random turns, marveling at his own stupidity. In a moment of panic, he stopped on a bridge on a rural back road and tossed the pistol into the black stream below.

He asked himself over and over how he could convince himself that there was really supposed to be fifty thousand dollars in cash in that car. The dope dealers were stupid, but they weren't *that* stupid. He knew that now, should have known it then. But he got greedy. He nodded at his own eyes in the rearview mirror to confirm the thought.

Jesus, what was I thinking?

He stared at the tops of pine trees, backlit by the pink sunrise. He saw a brown sign for Bankhead National Forest and turned in the direction the arrow pointed. He followed the signs along ever-narrowing roads into the forest, where sunlight had yet to reach. He stopped at a crossroads and cut off the lights. Darkness fell upon him like a mantle.

He tried to sleep and accomplished nothing but a sore back as images of blood and Ray falling dead ran through his mind like an endless horror movie with no soundtrack. After an hour, he gave up, cranked the car, and headed back to Mississippi, a pink morning sky behind him and long highway shadows to his front.

Distracted and exhausted as he was, he did not notice the deputy sheriff's car—or the fact that he had crossed back into Mississippi—until he saw the brown-and-white closing on him fast enough to tell him it wasn't a coincidence.

"Fuck!" he yelled, eyes on the rearview. He thought about flooring it and outrunning the deputy until he realized that his car barely ran, period. Outrunning anything faster than a skateboard was out of the question. That realization turned into a fear he'd never felt, a terror that sent tremors through his hands on the wheel and through his bowels. He squirmed as panic rose in him like boiling water, and he thought he might come apart, joint by joint, as the deputy hit his blue lights and blasted the siren, one short whoop. He was caught, and he was fucked. He slowed, then pulled to the side of Highway 12, and came to a stop on a low shoulder covered with Johnsongrass and dandelions.

Already the cop was out of his car, shotgun at his shoulder and yelling at him to step out of the car. He killed the engine and rolled down the window. Stuck both hands through.

"It's going to be a long fucking day," he said to no one in particular.

COLT

H e waited for the buzz, then yanked the heavy steel door open. Stepped inside the corridor leading to the cell block and nodded first at the deputy behind the glass, then at John, who was walking toward him.

"How long you been here?" he said when John got close enough.

"Long enough to hear Mr. Delmer Blackburn in there freak the fuck out."

"Yeah?" He started toward the row of cell doors. "Well, I got to be honest. You'd scare the hell out of me, too, if I didn't know you."

John grinned and shook his head. "Yeah, well. That may be true, but Delmer looks like he hasn't slept in days, wants a lawyer, but can't stop talking. Even after I read him his rights."

"Let me guess," he said as he stopped at another steel door, the one that led to the interview room. "He didn't do shit, officer."

John snorted and pulled the door open. "Hear it for yourself."

He stepped into the room, and John clicked the door shut behind him.

Delmer Blackburn sat at the table in the center of the room, left hand cuffed to a metal rail than ran the length of the table. He looked like hell. Disheveled and jumpy as a cat. Maybe thirty, about one sixty. Skinny, with baggy clothes—at least the denim short-sleeve shirt. Completely unremarkable pale face and eyes, unruly blond hair. Delmer looked like half the males in the county.

He pulled out the empty metal folding chair and watched Delmer jump at the sound of the legs scraping the concrete floor.

Seated, he looked across the table. Delmer had a hard time looking him in the eye.

"Hell of a way to start a morning, ain't it, Delmer?"

All that produced was a shrug.

"You want some coffee? I'm sure I could find you a cup somewhere."

"Naw, man, I don't need no coffee."

He nodded and leaned his elbows onto the table. "Ahite then, let's just get to it. Deputy Carver told me he already read you your rights, and you understand them. That right?"

Delmer cleared his throat and crossed his arms. "Hell yeah, and I want a lawyer, 'cause I ain't done nothing anybody wouldn't a done."

He held up a hand. "I hear you, Delmer, and we already put a call in to the public defender's office. I'm going out on a limb and guessing you can't afford an attorney."

Delmer shook his head and looked genuinely nervous.

"Right," he said. "So I imagine ol' Gideon Hayes is breaking every speed limit in town to get here. As far as them two dope dealers—the dead ones—I'm sure I follow your logic. I mean, I think the last robbery kinda went sideways on you, right? Shit got out of hand, bullets flying, all that?"

Delmer shrugged. It seemed to dawn on him that his best course of action was to keep his mouth shut.

He leaned a little more across the table, made sure Delmer locked eyes with him.

"But those other two guys, you killed," he said, watching Delmer's face. "Those two I can't figure out."

Delmer's eyebrows shot up, and he jerked so hard the cuff on his wrist rattled against the rail. "What other two?" he said.

He stared at Delmer. The guy was not real bright and seemed incapable of guile. But so did a lot of other murderers. He leaned back in his chair. "Oh, come on, Delmer, you're not going to sit there and tell me you didn't kill Pritchard and Munny."

"Hell no, I did not," Delmer said, all puffed up and offended by the accusation. "I knew they was dead, I mean I heard they was dead, but I sure as shit didn't kill them."

"Delmer, I think that's bullshit. Right now I got four dead drug dealers in this county. You're all but confessing to killing two of them, and you robbed the other two. I'm willing to bet you killed Pritchard and Munny. What I want to know is how and why."

Delmer sucked in half the air in the room, his eyes wide with terror.

"Sheriff, I swear 'fore God I didn't kill Pritchard and Munny. And that shit on the highway, that was self-defense. They came out that car packing all kinds of artillery. OK, I ripped Pritchard and Munny off, but I didn't kill 'em."

"See, now we're getting somewhere. Where did you rob Pritchard?"

"About two blocks away from Winnie's, man. I hit his ass hard and fast and got out of there. That sumbitch fought back, too."

"And look where it got him. What about Munny?"

"In his apartment. I broke in and took what he had there."

"And both of them were alive when you left them?"

Delmer looked at him like was an alien. "Well, yeah, of course they were. I sure as shit didn't kill them."

He leaned into Delmer again. "Then who did?"

"I ain't got no idea."

"Bullshit."

"I don't know," Delmer yelled in a panicky, girlish voice.

He stood and walked to the wall, facing Delmer, and began pacing.

"Delmer," he said, "here's the situation. You're facing two counts of murder, possession, hell, grand larceny, and whole bunch of shit I haven't even thought up yet. Your ass is going down for that."

Delmer sagged in his chair and lowered his head to the metal table, and for a moment, it looked like he was going to cry.

He stopped pacing and leaned against the wall. "So my question to you, Delmer is do you want to help yourself?"

Delmer made a noise that sounded like a yes, if a cat could say yes.

"Look at me."

Delmer raised his head.

"What in the hell were you thinking?"

Delmer put his head in his hands. "You think I ain't been asking myself that same damn question all fucking night?"

He crossed his arms. "I've heard of stupid shit before, and this is right up there."

Delmer snorted through this hands. "Oh yeah, sure, easy for you, when you're the law around here. Local boy, football star, badass Marine. Yeah, you know a lot about my options, don't you? You know what I was thinking? One big score, and me and my mother would finally be free of the goddamn suffocating misery that both of us are in. Who knows, maybe we could get the fuck out of here and this miserable shithole town.

"You ain't got no idea what it's like growing up without a father and a mother who's a drunk and a drug addict."

"I got an idea. What happened to your father?" he asked, still leaning against the wall.

"I's too young to remember the man when he died," he said. "Car wreck over in Starkville, so my momma says."

"Where is your momma?"

"How in the hell should I know? She never got over it and started drinking and drugging because of it. And she did that shit for years."

"Did? She sober now?"

Delmer nodded and wiped his nose with the back of his hand. "Yeah, supposably, but not that it makes any difference at all. Fucking moody and needy all the time. I ain't got time for that. Shows up when she needs money, disappears for months at a time. Called me a month ago to say she was sober, but who the fuck knows, you know? I don't have any idea how to handle her. Tried to get her to take medication, you know, go see a shrink or something, but she won't do it.

"So, to answer your fucking question, what was I thinking? I was thinking I'd get the fuck out of this hellhole and take my mother with me."

He pushed himself away from the wall. "Well, if you still want to have even a hope of a chance to help your momma, you listen good. Somebody is running around killing people in my county. The same people you stole from. And you're going to help me find him. Or you do the whole stretch for double murder, and you can forget about ever helping your mother. Understand?"

A single, shining silver tear crept down Delmer's right cheek. His head barely moved through a nod. "Where's my damn lawyer?"

He turned and knocked on the door. "No idea. Ain't called him yet." He stepped into the corridor where John waited with his hands in his pocket and a bored look on his face.

"You hear any of that?"

John nodded. "Some. Told you he won't shut up."

"'Cause he's scared shitless. But I don't think he's the guy I'm looking for."

"You serious?" John wasn't bored anymore.

He nodded. "Yeah, he's an idiot, and he's got issues, but he ain't the type to go around shooting people in the eyes with snake shot."

"Snake shot again?"

He nodded. "Yeah, Freddie Mac confirmed it. Two shots to the eyes. And that shootout on the highway didn't involve snake shot, I can guarantee you that. I think somebody is killing these guys after Delmer robs them."

"Why? And who?"

"Don't know, at least not yet. Munny and Pritchard ran dope for McNairy, though. My guess is the McNairy bosses got a little pissed off about the robberies and decided to set an example."

"Wait. Wouldn't it be easier to kill the guy doing the robberies? Why not kill Delmer?"

"They probably didn't know it was Delmer. At least until last night. They set him up, and it went to hell when they did try to kill him."

"So what do we do?"

He started walking toward the exit.

"Call Gideon and tell him he's got a new client. Then we're going to let him go."

John grabbed his arm. "Whoa. Let him go? He's a murder suspect, Colt."

"I know. Best one we got. But if my theory holds, this McNairy asshole will keep gunning for Delmer in there. Maybe the other person who got shot out there on Highway 12 was this McNairy guy. So, we let Gideon think he's getting sprung on a technicality, see if he can lead us to the guy. And when he does, we'll snatch his ass."

John sighed. "I don't know, Colt. Sounds risky. And not very solid."

"Yep. On both counts. But I got a hunch. Besides," he said as he stepped through the steel door back into the jail lobby, "it beats the hell out of campaigning."

MOLLY

"Questions, sir?"

She allowed herself a breath of relief as she watched her boss, Timothy Rollins, mull over the data she'd just presented via a PowerPoint slide deck and a wall map of the area in question. Rollins, the special agent in charge of the Memphis office, had a habit of absorbing the information of an entire brief with very few, if any, questions until the end, whereupon he would rattle off a series of interrogatives, some general, others impossibly penetrating.

She had just delivered a kickass brief, she told herself. She had been meticulous with her chronology and careful to leaven her hunches with enough circumstantial evidence, physical evidence, and field agent acumen to make these hunches sound more like educated guesses.

She'd even chosen her attire with care and precision: a tailored black suit with a ultra-white shirt, simple gold necklace and earrings. She had worn it on only two occasions: when she was presented a commendation during her first tour in Memphis and when she first met the director of the bureau in Washington, DC.

Rollins sat quiet for another minute, fingers steepled under his chin, brow furrowed. She stood patiently across the table from him, whiteboard at her back. Then he sat up and put his elbows on the conference table at which he sat.

"First of all," he said in a baritone drawl that belied the executive suit and expensive watch. "That was an outstanding brief, Molly. Very thorough. And I like the logic behind your assumptions."

She nodded. "Thank you, sir."

"I do think, though, that the theory that this shooter is a serial killer may be a reach."

"I understand, sir," she said. Her face remained placid, but the faint and familiar sting of disappointment hit home.

"That's some damn good investigative work to find that link, but right now that link doesn't trump the preponderance of evidence and indications that this is a drug case. So I'm not sure about your task force proposal."

She nodded again, even as she felt her carefully constructed case collapsing. "Yes, sir, that's a valid point. But while I was doing the research for this brief, there was another shooting. Same general area."

"Really?" Rollins said. "And you think they're related?"

She nodded. "Possibly. Shootout on a rural highway two nights ago. Two dead. That one was all over the local news channel as a drug deal gone bad. One wounded, and my guess was it wasn't the shooter. I have a copy of the local sheriff's report if you want to see it."

She reached for the stack of papers on the table, but Rollins waved her off. "Keep going," he said.

"There was blood trail leading off into the woods from two dead bodies around a vehicle. No money or drugs. Brass all over the road. Nine millimeter and forty-four Magnum. Slugs in the bodies or embedded in the asphalt."

"Seems exactly like a drug deal gone bad," Rollins said. "And none of your snake shot?"

She shook her head and frowned. "No, sir, and I'll grant you that this might be an unrelated incident. But, still, the issue of the snake shot shooter nagged at me. Until I realized I'd heard of it before."

Rollins cocked an eyebrow. "How so?"

"I had to dig through some files to find it, but two years ago, a house fire in Knoxville. Cause remained undetermined, even after local fire department, ATF and even FBI investigations. House burned nearly to the ground. The female body, or what was left of it, wasn't found until two days later.

"The woman's remains were charred so badly it was impossible to determine time of death or much else, but one discovery was unmistakable to the examiner: the corpse contained small steel pellets in the skull, as if she had been shot through the eyes."

Rollins ran a hand along his chin, thinking.

"It's a long shot, I know, sir," she said, trying to get the words out before Rollins shut her down. "Because it was a fire presumed at first to have been caused by an explosion of some sort, ATF had investigated. My thought process was that since we found this case, we still have jurisdiction, and, more to the point, if that death was connected to the other two, it means that whoever this Snake Shot Shooter is, he's more than an enforcer or a warlord making a move on someone's territory. He was in all likelihood a serial killer." She stopped talking, held her breath, realizing just how batshit crazy this must sound.

"Molly, I'm not minimizing your work, and you have done some exceptional investigating. But this sounds like a drug case to me."

"Yes, sir. But since we—I—found it, even though I agree it's really a drug case, we have jurisdiction on the Knoxville fire. A task force would at least give us a chance to nail this guy."

"Molly, have a seat," Rollins said.

Uh oh, here it comes. She sat and forced her face to remain neutral even as anger roiled behind her eyes.

Rollins leaned forward again. As always, she was surprised at how young he looked up close and that he was more handsome than most agents his age. But her admiration ended there. His face, unlike hers, was not a mask. His was an expression that made him appear exactly as he was—a senior agent about to give her bad news.

"I know you want this," he said, looking her in the eyes. "I know what it's like to be behind the eight ball."

He must have seen her eyebrows rise, because he nodded, his mouth a tight line, brown eyes peering from under his brows.

"Fifteen years ago wasn't that far back," he said. "But even then, to be a black kid from Macon, Georgia, a rookie agent in this bureau..." He shook his head to punctuate the sentence. "I used to have a saying: Every damn day. That's what it was like. It took me two solid years in the Kansas City office just to get acknowledged. And that was because I managed to screw up on the first real case I contributed to. It wasn't a big case, or an important one. Some local liquor store owners running a back-door bootlegging operation. But I broke the chain of custody on some evidence—invoices of all things, if you can believe it."

She nodded. Didn't know what else to do. She was totally unaccustomed to someone as senior as an SAIC being this candid.

"Yeah, hosed it right up. So, a lot of charges dropped. Along with what little reputation I had. But I got past it. Just to have to put up with more bullshit every time I got an assignment with more responsibility.

"I read your file, Molly. The whole thing. You made a judgment call—you went with your gut. And in the end, you were right. That Stuart guy had a bead on those guys and what they wanted to do. You looked at the pieces, just like you did here. They stole weapons, killed one of their own, and tried to shoot down a freaking seven forty-seven. And would have, had you not put a bullet through Rodney Spears's head. You did the right thing."

"Thank you, sir," she heard herself say, without a shred of embarrassment.

"I know the breaks haven't come your way," he continued. "I don't know why. Other than you made some people in the bureau look like they dropped the ball. Not your fault. Maybe they did. And you can believe me when I tell you that when the opportunity comes for you to be in the lead, I'm going to give it to you. But this is not it. This belongs to the DEA. I'd like you to give them the same brief and be the sole liaison for our office, but I'm going to have to say no to organizing a task force."

Even though he had softened the blow, and even though she took him as sincere, she fought down a lava fountain of rage and resentment. It wasn't fair, no matter how much Rollins tried to empathize and pay her due respect and promise to watch out for her. Fuck that. She had busted her ass on this, and she'd be goddamned if she'd stand in front of a room full of smirking cowboy DEA assholes fucking her with their eyes.

She nodded. "Yes, sir. I understand, sir. May I make a request?"

He nodded. "As long as it's not a request for a transfer."

She forced a smile. "No, sir. But I pulled some pretty serious hours pulling all this together. Would it be OK if I took a couple days of leave? I could use the break, and I'd like to go back to Virginia and visit my parents."

Rollins's dour expression melted into one of relief. "Absolutely."

"Thank you, sir," she said. "I'll pack all this up." She stood, as did Rollins.

"Good job, Molly," he said as he left the room.

She nodded, her mouth clamped shut.

DEE

He limped out the front door and squinted into the glare outside. The Percocet was still buzzing in him, but the sun hurt his eyes as he walked to the rental car.

He cranked up, hit the A/C at full blast, and pulled out onto the small asphalt road that fronted the house. He hoped this wouldn't take all day. He had only a couple of Percocets in his pocket and his leg still hurt.

He rolled into town and turned left into a drive-in restaurant. Hit the power window switch while he read the menu, and when the dude came on the intercom, he ordered the first meal he saw—burger, fries, soda combo.

He wasn't there for the food. He had a name, and his job today—as ordered by Hack—was to learn all he could about one Delmer Blackburn. Which shouldn't be hard. He had a wad of cash, and he could sniff out dope fiends from a mile off. The good dealers always can.

That cowboy motherfucker Turn had hung out at this joint, before he got his dumb ass shot. Dee looked the place over, with its faded yellow awnings, dirty parking spaces, shitty intercom, and bored-looking staff and decided this was a natural fit for that gunslinging idiot.

His food arrived, on a tray carried by a skinny teenage boy with dull eyes and acne. Brown hair shooting out from under a red visor.

"Hey, man," he said to the boy, "you see Turn around here? He flashed a grin, then went serious, for effect.

The kid knitted his brow at him, more curious than alarmed. Then shook his head.

"Dude, Turn's dead," the kid said. "Got killed a couple of days ago."

"What?" he said. "No shit? What happened?" He handed over a ten for the lunch and pulled the greasy sack into the car.

The boy shrugged. "Dunno. Cops said drugs or some shit. He got shot over on 12."

He feigned a puzzled look.

"The highway northeast of town, toward the state line," the boy said.

"Oh." He nodded. "Well, damn, I'll have to read 'bout that in the paper." He took his change. "Hey, you know any his buddies? I came outta Memphis to see him, and I at least could, you know, say hey to his people."

The kid thought. "Only friend of his I know is Alan Ross."

"Where he hang?"

Another shrug. "He works at the Home Depot on 45."

"Hey, man, thanks, I'll stop by." He took another ten out of his pocket and handed it to the kid, whose eyes went wide.

"You already paid," the kid said.

He nodded. "I know. That's for you. Tip for being friendly."

The kid glanced over his shoulder at the restaurant. Inside, three more teenagers busied themselves with orders for the half dozen other cars parked in stalls around the building. He smiled. "No problem."

He found Alan Ross in the paint aisle at Home Depot. Ross was older than the drive-in kid and seemed to know why he was there. That allowed him to cut through the bullshit. It cost him a fifty and two Vicodins, but he got more info on Delmer

Blackburn. He was sure to drop enough hints to let Ross know that Blackburn was in deep shit with a bad motherfucker from Memphis.

"You tell him," he said to Ross, "he want to parlay, he should hit me up." He handed Ross a slip of paper with the number of the burner phone he used for such purposes.

"Yeah, sure, man," Ross said, a little unsure of what to make of this information.

He spent the next three hours repeating this routine, crisscrossing the county, chatting up dealers, users, and bartenders. It cost him nearly $400 plus half a dozen pills, but it wasn't his money or dope anyway. Plus, he was the one got shot. He figured the shit evened out.

Delmer Blackburn was just a small-town idiot. Worked several jobs here and there in town, lived with his mother for about a year, ever since he lost his job at the Dollar Tree and couldn't pay the rent. Then, the mother took off, disappeared. Blackburn had been bouncing around ever since.

Satisfied with the dossier, he headed back toward Columbus to complete the second task: to get the scoop on this Rhonda Raines woman. Hack had been adamant about that.

He had her address and place of work—courthouse downtown, which, if anybody cared to ask him, was pretty damn risky. But nobody, especially Hack, asked. He also had her license plate number. That shit with her son sounded bad. Drug deal that went south, sounded like. Shot by some white guy dealer. She still went to "grief recovery" meetings on a regular basis.

He slowed as he drove past the statue of a Confederate soldier on the corner of the courthouse lot. The courthouse itself looked like something out of *Gone with the Wind*—a towering brick building with huge white columns at the entrance and a clock tower.

Rhonda Raines was a court officer in that building, and even though he'd prefer to know a little more about where she did that work and when she left for the day, there was no way in hell he was stepping foot inside that building, not with a bullet hole in his leg and a pocketful Percocet. Instead, he rolled past the building and made several turns through downtown until he was reading address numbers off houses and mailboxes until he came to the one that matched the Raines woman.

He pulled to the curb. Her house wasn't much. One story, white, and needing a paint job. What little yard there was had mostly weeds and brown, dead spots. Same with the other houses in the area—he recognized it as the part of town where black folks lived, some trying to live a normal life of jobs, kids, and bills and the rest hustling.

He parked at the curb and limped up the low concrete steps to the front door. He tried the door a couple of times. Locked. He glanced around the neighborhood and thought about walking around back, but decided it was too obvious—plus he couldn't run for shit if it came to that. Instead, he climbed back into his car, dug a Percocet out of his pocket, tossed it in his mouth, and chewed it as he turned the car around. He headed for the church where the grief recovery meetings were held.

COLT

He couldn't help but smile. John and Gideon Hayes had been going at it for about twenty minutes out in the main office and so far agreed only on the fact that it was morning.

His pleasure at the scene, which he viewed from the relative safety of his office, was not without its guilt.

Technically, he should be the one having this conversation with Gideon, going over the particulars of the Calvin Bibb arrest. Hayes had jockeyed for the case as soon as he learned Bibb couldn't afford a lawyer and that, it being a federal case, he might get a little publicity.

But John had been first on the scene, and, anyway, a day avoiding Gideon Hayes, even if only for a moment, was a win. John would give him shit about it later, but he'd rather put up with that than one of Hayes's condescending, loquacious lectures— even though he knew he had one coming himself.

He watched the two over his coffee cup: John with his hands on his hips, jaw set, eyes hard. Hayes, ever haughty, in a cheap public defender suit, effete gestures, and tolerant attitude.

John cut his eyes at him, and he tried to hide behind his cup and the desk, but he caught the exasperated look in John's eyes. Yeah, he owed John a beer after this one. He set his cup down.

"Gideon," he called, beckoning for the lawyer to come.

Hayes snapped his head round, and he could see the relief in John's eyes. He tried not to grin.

Hayes walked in with his trademark gangly gait, a lot of arms and legs and a prominent Adam's apple. In a wrinkled brown suit that clearly came straight off the rack, he looked every bit the part of a shabbily dressed, modern version of Ichabod Crane, right down to the wrinkly forehead, huge nose, and ears too big to fit under a haircut that looked like a pile of hay.

"Good afternoon, Samuel," Hayes said as he came to a stop in front of the desk.

He gritted his teeth. "Gideon, how many times have I told you that nobody calls me that anymore?"

Hayes adjusted the crooked wire-rimmed glasses on his hawk-like beak and grinned. "And how many times have I told you that Samuel is the name you were born with, thus the name by which you should be called. I stand on the principle that men should be called by the name given at birth."

He scoffed. "Do tell. For somebody whose principles are as elastic as yours, that's an interesting one to stand on."

"Be that as it may, Sam—"

He held up a hand to cut him off.

"What's this I hear about you filing a motion to dismiss on Delmer Blackburn?"

Hayes huffed and put his hands on his hips in a very lawyerly show of exasperation. "Indeed I am," he said. "You scared him to death with a double murder charge, but you don't have anything to back it up."

He leaned back in his chair. "C'mon, Gideon, he all but confessed to shooting those two dealers not two hours ago."

"Outside the presence of an attorney," Hayes said. He crossed his arms and looked at him over the top of his cockeyed glasses. "You don't have a murder weapon. You don't have any drugs or money, or any proof that my client was even on the scene."

"I've got motive," he said. "And his lack of an alibi constitutes opportunity."

"Huh. That could be said for half the population of the county," Hayes said.

"And he had weed on him when we arrested him."

Hayes grinned. "So all you have is a possession charge."

He stared at Hayes. The man had no idea he was acting according to plan. He stared out the window to give Hayes the impression he was struggling with a dilemma. Finally, he said, "Dammit, Gideon, I hate to say it, but you're right. I can't hold him or charge him with murder—not yet—but I'm going to charge him with possession. You can figure out jail with the judge."

Hayes beamed and flung his arms open in triumph. He looked like a skinny, ugly bird of prey. "Of course," he bellowed. Then, with a lowered voice, "Although, part of me would have thoroughly enjoyed ripping apart this flimsy case of yours."

"Get out of my office, Gideon. Go see to your scumbag client."

Hayes smirked, did an about-face and loped out of the office past a scowling John.

He waited until Hayes was completely out of sight before he smiled. Fucking lawyers.

On the desk, one of the lights on his phone blinked. He ignored it, set the cup down, and turned to his computer screen. He had his own work on the Bibb case to finish and submit to the feds.

An hour later, Becky leaned into his office. "Colt," she said. "Line one."

He looked up, nodded, and took the call. "Harper."

"OK, Sheriff, it's me, Delmer. I'm calling just like you said to."

"Glad to see you cooperating," he said.

"So, uh, what next?"

"Well, for one thing, don't try to rip off any more drug dealers. Go home and sit tight. I'll let you know when I need you."

He hung up and turned his attention to a pile of paperwork Becky had left for him, mostly reports and requests that required his signature.

DELMER

After he hung up with Harper, he listened to the voice mail from Ross again, and looked at the number he had scrawled on a paper towel in his kitchen.

"Hey, Delmer, it's Alan Ross, man. I just ran into some guy from Memphis, black guy, looked like a thug, and he was real interested in you. Said something about you having pissed off a cold-blooded guy who could be dangerous to your health. I'm not making this up. Said you could fix things if you wanted, but you better do it quick. He left me a number—"

He ended the call, deleted the message. He should have told Harper about it, but at the last second he decided not to. Harper didn't give a fuck about him and would probably just burn his ass anyway after he caught up to whoever killed Pritchard and Munny.

There may be an angle to work here, he thought. *If I can just figure out what it is.*

COLT

He read the newspaper story about the Munny homicide—it wasn't nearly as lurid as the story about Pritchard being fished out of the Luxapalila—over a barbecue plate at Sally's on Catfish Alley.

When he finished and had overtipped Sally, he walked the three blocks to the courthouse, even though the humidity made it feel more like a swim.

He managed to make it to the steps of the stately, columned courthouse building without completely sweating through his uniform shirt, but he still said a prayer of thanks for conditioned air when he heaved on the heavy tinted-glass door and stepped into the cool, dark interior. He nodded at the security guard who waved him around the metal detector and made his way down the wide corridor past people who spoke in whispers on account of the fact they were in the seat of the county government.

He went through a green glass door on his right and found Rhonda at her desk in a cubicle, her brow furrowed as she clacked on her keyboard and scowled at the screen over her cheap plastic reading glasses. He draped his arms over her cubicle wall and smiled.

"Nice glasses," Ms. Raines.

"Sheriff Harper," she said without looking up, "that comment is dangerously close to harassment, which could have an effect on your reelection campaign—if you ever start one."

He put his hands up in mock surrender. "The department apologizes for the insensitive comments of the sheriff."

She shook her head and laughed, then snatched the glasses off her nose. "Colt, what are you doing?"

"I was in the area."

"Right."

"Just wanted to see how you're doing."

She laced her fingers in her lap "Thank you. I'm fine."

"Still going to your meetings?" he said in a low voice.

She nodded. "They help. Wouldn't hurt you to go, either."

He scoffed. "The last thing I feel over Winston is grief."

She looked down. He looked around the cube farm at the tops of heads, all busy with the business of the county. He cleared his throat.

"Anyway," he said, "I just wanted to make sure you're doing OK. How's John?"

She looked up at him, surprised. "You're asking me? You work with him every day."

"That's not what I was asking."

She leaned forward on her desk and drummed her nails on the space bar on her keyboard. "He's fine. Worried a little about you, just like me."

"Worried about me? What did I do?"

She looked around the room, then back at him. "Colt Harper, this is not the place to have personal conversations. Now, if you'd like to stop by and visit every so often, or even at all, I'd be happy to tell you all the things about you that worry me."

He smiled; at this point, it was his only defense. "OK, OK, I'll stop by."

"Soon."

"Yes, soon. Get back to work."

She arched an eyebrow. "Take your own advice, Sheriff," she said. And smiled.

As he came down the sidewalk, he noticed a tall man in a blue suit approaching. He knew most of the lawyers in town, but this wasn't one of them, and even the ones he knew certainly didn't wear suits as expensive looking as the one coming toward him. Cuff links glittered under the sleeves and his brown shoes gleamed. When he got closer, he noticed the man's eyes more than anything else. Laser-beam blue, cold and steady. The stranger walked right down the middle of the walk.

He stopped four feet from the man.

"Sheriff Harper, I presume," the man said.

"I am," he said. Deep in his brain, a quiet alarm sounded. "And who might you be?"

Mr. Blue smiled—big, white teeth. "My identity is irrelevant for your purposes, Sheriff, but you may address me as Hack."

He studied the man's smile, thinking he could have easily just said, "My name is Hack."

"What can I do for you, Mr. Hack?"

The smile dimmed one notch. "I believe you are in possession of something of great value to me."

"You're going to have to be more specific."

"I believe you made an arrest this morning."

He nodded. "You mean Delmer Blackburn? Yeah, I arrested him. But I had to let him go."

Hack's eyebrows rose. "Oh, really?"

"Yes. Technicality. Let me guess, you were hoping to represent him."

Big smile from Hack. "Something like that. Well, Sheriff, I hope you'll forgive the intrusion."

He stood, waiting for Hack for step aside. He noticed that, even with the sun directly overhead, Hack did not appear to be sweating one drop. The man just stood there, blue eyes holding steady on his, grin fixed in place. The odd encounter was turning into an annoyance.

"Is there something else you want, Mr. Hack?"

A slight shake of the head. "Perhaps some other time, Sheriff." He stepped back and turned to go back from where he had come.

"I'll be waiting," he said.

He watched Hack walk down the sidewalk, two blocks, without looking back.

Arrogant fucking lawyers.

He pulled his cell from shirt pocket and dialed Blackburn.

"Delmer, you know a guy named Hack?" he said when Blackburn finally answered.

"No, why?"

"I just met him at the courthouse. Said you were something of great value to him. You have any idea what he's talking about?"

"Hell no. Like I said, I never even heard of the guy."

"If he contacts you in any way, you let me know."

"OK, Sheriff, no problem."

He hung up and walked away from the courthouse, his mind fumbling with a piece of information that didn't seem to fit. He stopped at his car, dialed John.

"John, I need you to run a name for me."

"Sure, Colt, what you got?"

"Look for a male, midthirties to early forties, named Hack or some variation. May be just a nickname, but run it anyway. At first I thought he was a lawyer."

"Got it. Any particular reason?"

"Could be nothing, but I got a weird feeling that I just ran into the guy killing the dope dealers in the county."

When he walked back through the office bullpen, John was banging away on a computer keyboard. John glanced up and nodded as he walked past and into his office.

An hour later, he was staring out the window at the cemetery when John came in reading from a sheet of paper.

"Fresh off the presses, boss," John said. "Nothing under Hack, but there's an interesting sheet on a Lewis Hackett, born McQuady, Kentucky."

"Jesus, where the hell is that?"

"Looked it up. Western Kentucky coal country. Hackett, thirty-eight, apparently did some juvie time, records sealed. Arrested for possession when he was eighteen, got probation. Then, a few months later, he killed a man in Cincinnati, did three years for manslaughter at Lake Erie Correctional Institution."

He turned and faced John, who was still reading off the sheet. "I didn't know there was such a place."

John looked up. "Oh yeah. Even guys in Chicago know what a shithole that joint is. Medium-security, maximum deathtrap."

"You're still reading. What else?"

"Five years ago, arrested for attempted murder. Knoxville. Charges dropped. Same with an aggravated assault charge in Memphis two years ago."

He sat on the window sill and shook his head. "This guy was wearing a suit that would cost me a paycheck. And this is the same guy?"

"Apparently so."

"How'd you get this so fast?"

John grinned. "Made a friend in Jackson last year when we were trying to run ballistics on that gun that killed Clifford Raines."

"Yeah? What's her name?"

"Rita. This guy, if it's the same guy, supposedly has ties or has had ties to crime bosses all over Tennessee and a few in Kentucky. Drug dealers, mostly."

"McNairy?"

John shrugged. "Don't know. Last known address was Memphis."

He walked back to his desk and flopped into his chair. "So maybe the rumors are true. This guy is a Memphis hitter sent down here to discipline some low-level dealers for being sloppy."

John slid the sheet across his desk. "Maybe so," he said. "That'd be my bet, anyway. So, now what do we do?"

He pulled the paper toward him, spun it around and read it over. "Stick with our plan. If that's why he's here, he's not leaving without the money Delmer has. He needs something to take back to his bosses."

HACK

He walked the length of the blazing hot street knowing that Harper was likely watching his every step. At least, that was his hope. To get Harper's attention. The news of Blackburn's release surprised him, but it also boded well. The sheriff himself was another matter. Seldom did he face a man who exuded equal amounts of confidence and hostility. Perhaps he'd spent too much time of late dealing with the dregs—the drug dealers, addicts, and the various lowlifes that populated the empire of Mr. Brooks. Harper, he surmised instantly, could be dangerous. Managed, certainly, but dangerous nonetheless.

Confident Harper was no longer watching him, he turned right and walked half a block in the shade of two brick buildings. He punched Dee's number up on his cell phone and told him of Blackburn's release.

"Find him," he said. "I want him to bring the money to us. Twenty-four hours."

He hung up before Dee could answer and speed-dialed Brooks's Memphis office. The receptionist put him through when he identified himself.

"Yes?" Brooks said from what sounded like a speaker phone.

"I will recover the money within twenty-four hours," he said.

"Good," Brooks replied. "Anything else?"

He smiled into the phone. "Actually, yes. It concerns the sheriff here."

"I'm listening," Brooks said.

COLT

He laid the rod on the deck, then stood and stretched his arms over his head while the boat drifted atop the sluggish black current of the Tombigbee. He craned his neck skyward to work out the kinks, and he gazed at a cobalt afternoon ceiling that warned him of thunderstorms later.

The impending storms did not faze him. Quite the opposite. As a boy, he would sit on the back stoop or a sidewalk or sometimes in a soybean field and await the violence and splendor that always followed the dimming of the light, the quickening breeze that carried the intoxicating scent of rain. His senses had always been keen to the changing moods of summer days, and today those senses told him the tempest was still distant.

He toed the control of his trolling motor and hopped into the cockpit. He had trolled his way up an almost-forgotten stretch of the old river, a convoluted channel that coursed through a series of limestone bluffs and deep hardwood forests. The Tennessee-Tombigbee Waterway, a few hundred yards to his left behind an impenetrable wall of trees and canebrake, gouged a straight channel through the river's ancient bends, sandbars, and eddies and reduced the current to a sleepy crawl while monstrous barges laden with coal and scrap iron chugged through a series of locks that connected the Tennessee River to the Gulf of Mexico. An engineering marvel forty years in the making, the waterway created a playground for boaters, skiers, and watercraft of all kinds. But it also wrecked hundreds of habitats for bass—unless you knew the still-pristine spots on the old river.

He'd been fishing this river for years, and while he groused about the loss of some of his favorite spots when the Tenn-Tom opened, he was surprised to find a few places that resulted from the dredging and digging.

He steered the boat with one hand while his eyes scanned the banks and water's edge. Sunlight seeped through the canopy of trees overhead, casting a greenish hue on the dark water. He kept to the middle of this narrow stretch of river so as to avoid the water moccasins he knew lurked in the willows at the muddy bank, coiled around low limbs, awaiting prey.

He made a sweeping turn to his left—he still called it port—to avoid an archipelago of stumps and deadfall—the same spot that allowed him to fill his live well with bass an hour earlier—and opened up the throttle under the lip of a bluff. The boat planed out and skimmed the glassy surface for fifty yards before bouncing into the chop of the main channel. He smiled in the sunlight, enjoying, as he had his entire life, the solitude and freedom of the river. It was his sanctuary, a place where he was most content. He would admit, though only to himself, that the river had a therapeutic, even spiritual, effect on him. After he'd come home from the war, he came here to think—and to escape. Sometimes to hide.

He summoned his mother's image and hymn. The only words he could remember besides the part about the everlasting arms had something to do with being safe and secure from all alarms, but he whistled the melody. He smiled in spite of himself. Today was a thinking day. The encounter with this Hackett asshole at the courthouse still nagged at him. He was pretty sure he killed Pritchard and Munny, even though he had jack shit for evidence, even with a rap sheet a mile long—something John pointed out more than once. But showing up the day Delmer got arrested sure seemed a hell of a coincidence. He knew that, in his heart of hearts, he just wanted to nail the guy. Hack's audacity had pissed him off, plain and simple. But there was more to it than that. Under the fancy suit and the perfect smile there seemed to be a malevolence that he could barely understand.

He pushed the throttle all the way open and hurtled the last two miles to the landing. Spray from the bow arched over and occasionally onto him, dousing him with droplets of respite from the heat.

When he saw the bait shop by the landing, high on the bank to his left, he cut the throttle and felt the boat settle onto her own weight for the slow drift to the ramp.

Only when he'd secured the boat to the trailer and pulled clear of the wet concrete did he open his tackle box and retrieve his phone. He turned it on and tossed it onto the seat of the truck.

He made it barely a mile before the phone vibrated its way across the seat. He grabbed it as he steered down the gravel road back to Highway 69. He saw John's name on the caller ID.

"What's up, John?" he said, squinting through the glare of the windshield.

"You do know this shit always happens when you're out of the office?"

"What now?"

"You remember Ms. Brinks? Cheryl."

"Uh, not particularly."

"That drunk woman at the store out on 69 a few weeks ago. Her husband came rolling up, and you backed his ass up."

He remembered. "Right. She drunk again?"

"It's her husband this time. He's gone batshit crazy. I mean, allegedly. He said he had a gun on his wife, then said something really bad might happen if he doesn't talk to you. In person. Like right fucking now."

He sighed and glanced at his boat in the rearview. *What the fuck?*

"He say what this was all about?"

"No, but Becky said he sounded drunk," John said.

"Of course."

"Of course."

"OK, I know you already sent a car," he said as he wheeled onto the blacktop, headed back toward town. "Tell 'em I'm on my way. And get on out there. I may need somebody covering me."

John chuckled. "Car's already there. Townsend is on scene. And I'm on the way to Caledonia."

"Figures he lives in Caledonia. Ahite, text me the address. Oh, and bring me a vest."

Another chuckle. "Sitting right here on the seat beside me."

"Of course. Be there in twenty."

"Roger."

He made it in a little under eighteen minutes, even pulling the boat. He felt a little ridiculous pulling up alongside two marked sheriff's cars.

The Brinks residence was one of the older ranch-style houses on the edge of town, built before the big tornado and before the huge influx of military personnel who came in a recent wave from the air force base to the north of town.

From the outside, the house looked normal: brick front, white trim, red door. Small covered porch with a white rail, carport with a deep freeze against the back wall, pickup parked inside. The standard shrubbery and flowers lining the concrete driveway to the street. Yard neat, grass mowed. Brinks, from the looks of it, didn't make a ton of money, but he wasn't broke, either.

He killed the engine and climbed out, aware that he smelled like fish and river water and looked like a redneck river rat, unshaven and dressed in jeans and a tank top. Hardly the image befitting a sheriff up for reelection.

If John noticed, he didn't let on. He strode around his own car, uniform on him like paint, sweat glistening on his arms and forehead. No hat, vest on, Glock holstered. John was cool. Always cool.

Townsend, an angular man of thirty with a harsh face and cold eyes, stood at the other car, behind his open driver's side door, eyes on the house as he spoke into his radio. Rifle with a scope laid out across the hood on a green mat. All business.

The moment flashed, and he was back in the corps, his squad in the desert, knowing their roles and staying frosty. All business. No time for fucking around.

He blinked himself back to the present and took the vest John offered. He shrugged into it, adjusted his holster and nodded. "So what's up? And do we really need a sniper?"

John shrugged. "Hell if I know. He'll scream out every now and then, hollering about wanting to talk to you. For all I know, we could have a hostage situation or a murder-suicide thing going on in there."

He squinted at the front door. *What gets into people? What in the hell can be this important?*

"Why in the hell couldn't he just call me direct?"

John shrugged. "Don't know. But he was pretty pissed that day at the store when I arrested his wife. And he seems a little unhinged right now."

"Well, I reckon I better go talk to Mr. Brinks. What's his first name?"

"Brad," John said. "Wait, boss, you just going to walk up there and knock on the door?"

He smiled. "That would be crazy. I'm going to yell at him first."

John shook his head. "Goddammit, Colt, one of these days."

"Yeah, I know. But not today." He turned to the house. "Mr. Brinks! Brad! It's Sheriff Harper. You mind if I come in and have a word?"

A thumping sound came from the house, and a curtain in the kitchen moved a fraction of an inch.

"Just you, Sheriff," Brinks yelled. "Nobody else."

"All right, Mr. Brinks. You should know that I'll be coming in armed. You understand?"

Silence. Then, "Yeah, I understand."

"Good," he said. "So I'd advise you to put down whatever weapon you might be holding and step away from it. I come in there and see you holding a weapon, I'm gone put you down, you hear?"

"Yes, sir."

He nodded. "Town, you got overwatch. I'm leaving the door open and I'll talk from there if I can. He pulls anything, you shoot his ass."

"Will do, Colt." Townsend was already behind the .30–06, draped across the hood of his car and squinting through the scope.

"John."

"I know," John said. "You'll feel me."

"I know I will." He patted the front of his vest for good luck, and John returned the gesture, an inside joke they'd shared since the Marine Corps. He drew his pistol and held it at his side as he walked to the front door.

He waited until he felt John behind him, off to his right just a little, then knocked. "Mr. Brinks, it's me," he said into the wood of the door. "Sheriff Harper." He kept the pistol low, but his fingers tingled around the grip.

The door swung open, and Brad Brinks filled the void so completely that Colt couldn't see past him into the darkened interior. Brinks was unarmed. Even so, he took a tiny step to his right to give Townsend a better shot, should he need to take it.

"Mr. Brinks," he said and nodded.

"Sheriff." Brinks's eyes were bloodshot and wary, almost feral, as the man seemed to try to see everything in the world at once. The smell of booze leapt from him, and he was clearly drunk. But, Colt noticed, he was also clearly scared. He barely resembled the brash husband who had considered, however briefly, challenging him in a parking lot a few weeks earlier. Gone were the boots, jeans, and attitude. He now wore battered, faded khakis and stood in his sock feet. Blue T-shirt. He seemed much smaller.

"Is Mrs. Brinks OK?" Colt asked.

Brinks nodded. "Yeah, she's fine."

"Is she safe?"

Another nod. "Yeah, she is. Weren't planning on doing something bad to her anyway. Though sometimes I sure as hell want to."

"That's not what we heard," he said. He considered his options and risks. He knew it best to keep Brinks in sight of his deputies, but he couldn't tell if Brinks was off his rocker or not. So he didn't know if the wife was really safe. Or alive. "Can you get her to come to the door?"

"Cheryl," Brinks called. "Get over here."

Cheryl emerged from the gloom of the interior in jeans and a maroon Mississippi State T-shirt. It occurred to him that he had never seen Mrs. Brinks in anything close to a relaxed state, much less happy. Her hair was brushed, and even though her makeup was fixed, it was clear she'd been crying.

"Ma'am," he said, watching her eyes. "Are you OK? Are you in danger?"

Her gaze held his. She was stone-cold sober, sane, and not under duress. It was his professional opinion.

"I'm safe, Sheriff," she said. She cut her eyes at her husband. "You tell him?"

He stood straighter, cocked an eyebrow at Brinks, who furrowed his brow, cleared his throat.

"Ain't had time. Go on now."

Cheryl didn't move. She returned her gray-eyed gaze to his own. He nodded. She disappeared into the interior of the home.

"Tell me what, Mr. Brinks?" He turned to John with a hand signal—*I got this.* John, standing in the front yard with his pistol drawn, lowered his aim. Townsend didn't twitch, not even to wipe sweat from his brow.

Brinks sighed. "Goddamn, I don't even know where to start."

"The beginning."

Brinks nodded. "Ahite then. I know this is going to get me in a shitload of trouble, but I ain't gonna stand around while people get killed."

"Go on."

"OK, OK, first off, though, I ain't no drug dealer. And I only tried that shit once, and it scared me so bad I said never again."

"Mr. Brinks."

"OK, OK," Brinks said, sweating like a glass of iced tea on a sunny porch. "I knew Kenny Jenkins, that guy you shot out to the lock and dam."

He tried to remain patient. "I remember Kenny."

Brinks nodded and sent a tiny shower of sweat flying off his brush-cut hair. "We hung out. I knew he was working for these guys up in Tennessee, and I figured he was doing a lot more than that 'enforcer' bullshit he said he was doing. Anyway, whatever, a while back, a few weeks ago maybe, some guy showed up where I work—over at the gas company—asking a ton of questions about Kenny. And you. Mostly you. Wanted to know how old you are, where you lived, if you had been investigating Kenny, if Kenny was a snitch, if you shot a lot of people, if you was married, and whatnot."

His inner alarm rang, loudly. He wondered if John was hearing this. He nodded at Brinks for him to continue.

"Well, hell, Sheriff, he was paying for the information, you know? I got bills."

"What did you tell him?"

"Not much more than he coulda gotten from reading newspaper, and that's the smoking hot gospel truth."

"OK, so what's the real problem?"

Brinks shifted his feet and blew out a breath. More sweat. "He, ah, he's been calling a lot lately. Since them guys started getting killed. Asking more questions about you. About your daddy. About that boy got killed last year."

He glared at Brinks. "Clifford Raines? What in the hell did he ask about him for?"

Brinks shrugged, and his eyes dove under his brows like a scolded child's. "Dunno, Sheriff, he just asked if you had a personal involvement in it, is how he put it."

"A personal involvement. What did you tell him?"

"I didn't know what to tell him, 'cause I don't know. I mean, I just read the papers, you know. I told him, it's a small town, you know everybody here, so, yeah, I guess that could mean a personal involvement."

"OK, so this moneyman, he tell you why he needed this information?"

"No, sir. Said was none of my business. In no uncertain terms. He was, ah, pretty scary."

"Is that why you called me?"

Brinks nodded. "Ever time I tried to be done with the guy, he'd get real nasty and tell me I was done when he said I was done, that sort of thing."

He fought to keep his face calm even as the anger boiled up inside him. *What the fuck does this guy want?* "That all you tell him?" he asked.

Brinks nodded. "Yeah, pretty much."

"So, other than being scared of this guy, why did you decide to tell me now?"

"I know them killings around here were all drug-related," Brinks said. "I ain't dumb. I can put two and two together."

"So? You said you ain't a drug dealer."

"I ain't," Brinks said, now on the defensive. "But, like I said, I hung out with Kenny. And Kenny had, um, friends who were dealing. I never met any of them or knew them by name, but I know one of them sounds a lot like that first guy that got killed. Pritchard? Yeah, that's him. And don't you think it's weird this guy is looking for you about the time all these dealers are showing up dead?"

He had the sensation of a puzzle assembling in his head as he merely watched the pieces come together. "This guy have a name?"

"Only one he gave was Hack."

"Hack."

"Yessir."

"Mr. Brinks, you're not suicidal, are you?"

"No, sir."

"Just scared."

"Yes, sir."

"OK, for now, you've done the right thing. My deputies might be contacting you real soon for more information, but for now, I'm going to go, all right?"

Brinks wore an expression of relief, fright, and confusion all melted into a sweaty red mess. "OK, then. But what do I do about this guy?"

"Don't piss him off." He turned and walked past a startled John. Townsend kept his rifle aimed at the door.

"Stand down, Townsend," he called from his car. The deputy immediately relaxed and unshouldered his rifle.

John caught up to him. "What the fuck, Colt?"

He beckoned for John to follow him to his truck, out of earshot from Townsend.

"John, look," he said. "Hackett—you remember him—has been asking questions and pumping Brinks here for info, asking about Kenny Jenkins and me. You still think he didn't kill Pritchard and Munny?"

"Well, that changes things a little," John said. "But I don't get it. You killed Jenkins over a year ago. That's a long time. And Jenkins was a real low-level thug."

"That's what I was thinking."

"Maybe he was asking about you to see what he'd be up against if he starts killing dealers. You know, could he count on local yokel sheriffs who couldn't do anything without tripping over their own dicks."

"Well, apparently, he felt like that was the case."

John looked at him. "Hey, Colt, all I meant was—"

"I know what you meant. This guy has balls. He killed Pritchard and Munny, knowing that I already shot one guy who worked for the same bunch.

"Allegedly," John said.

"Yeah, allegedly." He looked over John's shoulder at Townsend, who was backing his car out onto the street. "Look, I'm going to get ahold of Delmer right now and set up a meet with Hack."

"Roger," John said again and turned for his car.

MOLLY

She flung the beer bottle harder than she meant to. It hit the wall a good foot over the plastic trash can with a *thunk*, caromed off the desk and landed, spinning, at the foot of the bed in her Hampton Inn room off the interstate exit. She didn't bother to pick it up, such was her frustration. She continued to pore over the map spread out on the bed, as she had been for the last two hours, sitting cross-legged, notepad on the left, laptop on the right, beer in a Styrofoam cooler beside the bed. She was halfway through a six-pack.

She had driven from Memphis straight through to Lowndes County to test her theory and had found nothing. She'd made three educated guesses since her brief to Rollins as to where Pritchard's body could have been put in the water, and had walked away from all three sites with zero hints, just a lot of mosquito bites and the heebie-jeebies from a fear of snakes. She still had the bridges to check out—those still made more sense. She decided to regroup with rest, food, and beer. The only one she had neglected so far was rest.

Her map—a 1:50,000-scale military terrain map—offered damn little in the way of information other than terrain features and roads. She'd have to go out there and walk—or at least drive—the ground.

She stretched her arms over her head, then climbed off the bed, when she realized it was nearly midnight. She surveyed the pale yellow walls, riddled with nicks and smudges and wondered how in the hell she ended up here.

She was way out of bounds, she knew. Not breaking any laws or regulations necessarily, but sure as hell outside any authority she was supposed to answer to.

She felt a pang of doubt as the choices she had made rushed into her mind, reminding her that the line between winners and losers was paper thin—as even Rollins had alluded to during her brief. And the difference always could be reflected in the choices one made. She made hers, more than once.

She knew her decision to find this killer was reckless and had two apparent outcomes: she would be hailed as a gutsy, tough, smart investigator if she succeeded and a headstrong, reckless rogue agent if she failed. But she knew the only true outcome of this stubborn, defiant act was her own demise as a federal agent, by her own hand.

And having willfully painted herself into this corner, she saw but one recourse—to finish the job. Fuck the consequences. She would find either redemption or disgrace at the end of this journey.

And at the moment, she didn't care which.

DELMER

He got nervous after the third ring. He was ready to hang up when a voice came on the line.

"Yo, speak."

"Uh, yeah, who is this?"

"Depends. Who's talking?"

"Delmer. I got this number from—"

"That's enough, man. I know who you are. People been looking for you."

"So I hear. What do you want?"

The guy on the other end—he sounded black—laughed. "You a real piece of work. Me, I want a piece of yo' ass, motherfucker, for shooting me.

He closed his eyes and sat at his kitchen table. "Fuck," he said.

"Yeah, you right about that."

"What do you *want*?" he said.

"I know you ain't that dumb, but I'll spell it out. You got money don't belong to you. Me and my...associate want it back."

He stared up at the ceiling. His phone buzzed in his hand, and he saw he had another call coming in.

Shit, first this guy and now Harper.

He ignored the incoming call. "OK, I got your money," he said. "But why should I just hand it over?"

"'Cause you don't and Hack—my associate—is going to fuck you up."

"The way he did those other two guys?"

"Something like that."

He saw an opening. "Naw, man, y'all know I got the money, but you don't know where it is. I'll give it back, but I want something in return.

A snort from the other end of the call. "Oh, you want to bargain now?"

"That's right. I'll give you the money, and your associate lets me go anywhere I want to as long as it's not in this state."

"And why should he agree to that?"

"I just spent a few hours sitting in the sheriff's jail, and he's real interested in you and your associate. I'm sure he'd love to hear about this conversation."

"Hold on."

He drummed his fingers on the tabletop. He could hear voices in the background, probably discussing him. Or interesting ways to kill him.

"OK, look," the guy said when he came back on. "Here's how it's going to go. Hack says you bring the money tomorrow night. You tell us everything that sheriff has, give us the money, then get the hell out of the state. Just don't show up Memphis."

He breathed a sigh. "OK, deal. Where?"

"There's an old bridge just off of Highway 45 south of here."

"Yeah, I know it. Right after the four-lane goes back to two, down toward Brooksville."

"Whatever. Eleven o'clock tomorrow night. Money in a gym bag. Come alone. Park on the south side of the bridge. We'll come up from the north side and meet you halfway across."

"OK, I got it. What else?"

"Nothing. Don't fuck this up like you did the last time."

"Kiss my—" the connection broke.

His hands were shaking as he looked at his phone. He punched up Harper's number.

"It's Delmer," he said when Harper answered. "It's on."

"That was fast."

He told Harper about the voice mail and the conversation he had with Hack's "associate."

"I thought you said you didn't know this guy," Harper said.

"I don't. Other than I shot the guy I was talking to."

Harper scoffed. "Yeah, you really know how to make friends. So, details."

"No, not until I get some assurances."

"Assurances? Delmer, what assurances do you think you rate? You could be laying in the morgue with your eyes shot out right now."

"Yeah, and I may still be if this shit goes bad for me. I'll give you what you need, but you gotta assure me you'll leave me alone."

"And by leave you alone, you mean let you off for shooting those two dealers?"

"Yes."

Silence on the other end. Finally, Harper said, "OK, Delmer, here's my deal. Under one condition. This goes sideways—in any way at all—and I'll run your ass right back to jail. You hear?"

"Yeah, I hear."

"You help me get this guy, and I'll talk to Gideon about a lesser charge, something that gets you down to county time and probation. Deal?"

He still didn't like the sound of it, but he had no choice, really. "OK," he said. "Deal."

Ahite, so where's this going down?"

He passed the details to Harper, who said he'd call back when he was ready, then hung up.

He sat in his kitchen, breathing a little easier. He felt good about the situation now. He had a deal in place that covered his ass no matter what happened.

COLT

H e checked the map on his phone as he and John rolled down Highway 45, headed south toward the tiny town of Brooksville as the sun crept toward sunset. Long shadows fell across the roadway, breaking up the contours of the parched green hillocks that formed the east Mississippi prairie.

"So, what do you think?" he asked as John stared out the window at the wide green fields that opened up after they'd left town.

"That farming in this heat would suck."

He smiled. "No, I was talking about the plan."

John sighed. "Man, the plan is fine. It's all the rest I'm not sure about. I mean, what the fuck are we doing here, Colt?"

He shrugged. "Shit's personal now."

"According to one scared dope-dealing drunk and one scared thief."

"Brinks said he wasn't a dope dealer."

"Still."

"Still, I believed him," he said as he spun the wheel through a right-hand turn off Highway 45 onto a dirt road. The car bounced toward a sluggish brown gash of water, where an ancient metal truss bridge stood like an exhausted sentinel.

"Well, obviously," John said. "So, what are you thinking?"

He grinned and stopped the car on the north side of the muddy stream. "Let's recon this place, like we talked about. See if we can find an edge."

They climbed out of the car and walked the baked clay path to the bridge. Weathered, bowed planks ran its length in two rows. The rusted metal trusses were a relic from the original highway built decades earlier. The railings sagged in places, and leaned out over the creek in others.

"Motley Slough," he said, pointing at the water. "I'd forgotten this bridge was still standing."

John put his hands on his hips. He looked like a drill instructor in the wrong uniform. "Yeah, well, there ain't shit for cover or concealment out here," he said, squinting up and down the creek's path. He started down the crumbly dirt shoulder toward the thick foliage lining the water's edge.

"Watch out for snakes," he called as he started across the span, the planks creaking under his boots.

John swore and stepped back onto the road.

"Looks like a turnout there on the right," he said, pointing to the other side.

"Yep, and another on the left, closer to the bridge," John said.

He stopped on the south side of the bridge. "Delmer's going to be coming up this way. You're right, there's not much room to be stealthy. But," he said, waving a hand over the south bank, "we'd be below the line of sight right here."

"Sure," John said, "provided we get there without being seen. What about up there?" He pointed to a dirt track twenty yards ahead on the left, running from the dirt track into a stand of trees.

"We could use the trees for cover," he said, "but I'm not sure we could see anything or close the distance to the bridge in time."

John nodded again. "Good place for a handoff," he said. "One way in, one way out."

He walked back to the middle of the span. Cicadas screamed in the distance, announcing the coming evening. Below him, the creek barely moved, its current creeping past hardly noticed.

"Here's what I'm thinking," he said. "We get here around dusk—eight, nine o'clock, and park off in that low spot. We'll be out of sight, but we'll see Delmer go by. After Delmer parks, we'll use his car for cover—and it'll be dark as hell out here then—come up from behind."

They walked back to the car.

"It'll probably be two on two, from what Delmer said," he said as he cranked the car and John turned the A/C up a notch.

"And you trust what Delmer said?"

"It's all we got at the moment."

John sighed, then nodded. "You ever think the bad guys are doing the same thing we are, and coming up with their own plan? What happens then?"

He shrugged. "Well. Then we make it up as we go and hope the right people get shot."

He pulled back onto the highway, headed back toward town.

"Boss, are you sure you want to do this?"

"I don't have much of a choice anymore, John."

"The hell you say. There's all kinds of ways we can snag this guy."

He growled and shook his head. "The hell I don't. I don't know who this guy is or why he's after me—other than I shot a little dirtbag I went to high school with who happened to work for some two-bit redneck mob in Tennessee."

John lowered his head, a sure sign his temper was rising. "Other than that, no—no reason at all for him to come after you. If that's what he's actually doing. I mean, he was face-to-face with you. If he was after you, he missed a perfect opportunity."

He looked at the man who had been his closest friend for more than twenty years. "You doubting me?"

John looked out the window at the catfish farms flying past. "No, I'm not doubting you. Necessarily. I just think we—"

"What?" he said. "Have you forgotten this guy was asking about Clifford -- and maybe Rhonda?"

"That's a cheap shot, Colt," John said, crossing his arms and leaning back in his seat.

He sighed. "Yeah, maybe it was. But it's true."

"You're supposed to be running for reelection. You can't really be contemplating...whatever the hell it is you're contemplating."

He looked John in the eyes. "Only thing I'm contemplating is stopping this guy."

John frowned. "Just stopping him? I know you. You're going to have to be more specific."

"What part of stop do you not understand?"

John drew a sharp breath and pointed a finger at him. "Don't play that shit with me, Colt. We been through too much together for you pull that kind of crap on me."

He gripped the wheel with both hands. "John, this ain't about reelection or any other shit. This is about—"

"Justice?" John's tone had softened, but not his expression.

He stared at John. "No. This is personal. That's it."

John's eyes widened, and his face fell. "Dear God. Rhonda was right."

"What?"

"She said you're the kind who wants redemption but only understands violence."

He threw John a look. "The *fuck* are you talking about?"

John's eyes flashed angry. "Really? I think you want this guy to come after you. You might even need this guy to challenge you. That's what I think."

He sighed. The man had taken a bullet in the ear for him. Had kept confidences and upheld the bond of loyalty. They had been side by side for as long as he could remember. "I'm going to nail this guy. You in or out?"

"Just shut up and drive. Tomorrow night, it's me and you. Like always."

DEE

This is a real stupid idea, he thought. He sat behind the wheel of the car, which squatted on the side of a rutted dirt road, next to a darkened field of soybeans, between Highway 45 and the bridge.

Hack leaned against the hood of the car, his shoes crunching the gravel every so often. He just leaned, peering into the blackness, wearing a gray suit that must have cost a thousand dollars.

The whole drive out here, Hack had gone from silent to preaching some weird shit about being a beacon, drawing people to him so as to show them retribution and atonement for their sins. Or some shit like that. Then silent, then another fucking rampage about this asshole Delmer Blackburn, who was going to pay for his sins and crimes, and how he was going to do that.

The plan was simple. Hack would meet Blackburn halfway, take the money, shoot Blackburn, and dump him over the side of the bridge into the river.

But simple don't mean smart.

Doing this shit out in the open—even late at night on this country road—made him nervous. He liked the isolated spots better, like when ol' Mr. Freeze shot that dude out in the woods.

Hack made the calls, though. And he paid well. So he could talk all the crazy shit he wanted, and kill whoever he thought needed killing, sins or no sins. Long as he didn't get shot again, he was good with it. And he damn sure wasn't getting shot again. Not tonight.

He peered through the windshield's dirty film of dust and smashed bugs into the moonless night. A tree stood off in the soybean field, and one dead limb stretched out from the canopy of the healthy branches, a grotesque hand grasping at the black sky. He was a long way from Memphis.

JOHN

He drained the paper cup of bad coffee and set it on the floorboard of Colt's truck. To his right, across the bridge and into the black night, he knew there was trouble to be found. If he was sitting on a stakeout with Colt and not talking, he knew trouble was coming.

He looked across the seat at his boss. Colt, as usual, was cool, with his head back against the seat, eyes closed but still very alert. He'd never seen Colt *not* alert.

Outside, the bridge loomed black against the faint blue moonlight like the skeleton of some prehistoric beast. He stared at the span as if it were an electric chair or a gas chamber. Somebody would likely die on that bridge tonight, he thought. That's the only reason Colt was here. And, for that matter, himself. He and Colt had been in this spot before, and, on one occasion, he'd gotten half his ear shot off, a fact that remained something of a running joke between them.

I'm not scared, he told himself. And he wasn't lying. A little concerned about the unknowns, but not scared.

"So, regret shooting Kenny Jenkins now?" he asked in an attempt to lighten the mood.

Colt's eyes opened, and he glared at him. "Hell no. Jenkins had it coming. 'Course I never counted on all this shit happening."

"Yeah, good thing you don't like doing this kind of stuff."

Colt shot him a look. "Don't start with me, Carver."

"Yeah, yeah, I hear you. Delmer rattled on, didn't he? Back there at that gas station?"

"Yeah, I was a little worried he was too drunk and too scared to make it the rest of the way, or to even hear what I was telling him. But he seemed to pull it together when he finally grasped the idea that we'd be behind him when he got to the bridge here."

"You check him for a weapon?"

"Of course I did. You think I want that idiot carrying a gun?"

"Well, now, give him credit. He has killed two men."

Colt snorted. "Well, he ain't killing anybody tonight."

"Nope," he said, peering through the windshield. "He's scared to death of this guy. To hear him talk, this Hack cat is a brutal son of a bitch. And he sounds like a ghost."

"Ghost, my ass," Colt said. "Ghosts don't show up on bridges in the middle of the night demanding money." Colt sat up. "I don't give a damn if he's a ghost or a cheetah. Sumbitch wants to come after me, I'll make it easy for him.

DELMER

He remembered reading in a military history book—one of hundreds he read as a kid to try to learn something about his dead father—that men in combat nearly always suffered from a debilitating, seemingly unquenchable thirst, brought on by a level of fear—terror, really—that was difficult to understand for most people.

He was terrified now, and felt as if he would die from thirst. He'd stopped on the way out of town to get a liter of water at the Stop-N-Shop. The empty plastic bottle rattled on the floorboard on the passenger side. He hoped the water would also clear his head a little. He'd had too many shots of bourbon, so his head was a little fuzzy. He could hardly concentrate on what Harper was saying at the Stop-N-Shop, where they went over last-minute details.

He wished Harper would have let him have a goddam piece, something to defend himself with should that black guy get an itchy trigger finger. But Harper was a dick, one of those take-charge, my-way-or-the-highway assholes.

He sighed. But at least Harper had a plan. He tried to focus on that and the road as he drove toward the rendezvous, rather than the sense that the rendezvous would culminate with a bullet in his head.

Harper had laid it all out like it was some kind of military operation in a war movie. He and his deputy were already at the bridge, hidden off on the right side of the road in a spot Harper assured him wouldn't been seen from the other side.

His job was to follow Hack's instructions to get to the bridge. After he parked his car—and slammed the door hard enough for Harper to hear—he was to take the gym bag with the money and meet Hack halfway across the bridge.

While this was going on, Harper and Carver would walk up the shoulder of the highway until they got close to the bridge, then make their presence known.

Harper was going to do all the talking—naturally—and had made it clear that he intended to kill this Hack guy.

He heard a loud, rending noise in his car, then realized he was hearing his own sobbing. He clamped his mouth shut and gripped the steering wheel until his fingers went numb.

The car hummed down the dark highway that glowed like a pale gray ribbon shining in the gloom before falling away into darkness. The far edge of his headlights found the turnoff to the southern approach to the bridge, and he wheeled onto the dirt road, kicking up dust and sending bugs flying in all directions. As he closed on the bridge, a glint of light reflected from the right side—Harper's truck—and he hoped to God it wasn't visible from the other side.

Up ahead, across the creek on the side of the road, twin headlights blinked, then began moving toward him. His throat tightened as he watched Hack's vehicle make its way toward his own.

Once past Harper's truck—he didn't even throw a glance that way—he slowed, then stopped. The other vehicle did the same, but then swung into a U-turn and stopped facing the opposite direction—in the right-hand lane—at the far edge of the bridge.

He cut off his headlights and huffed out a foul breath. He held on to the steering wheel to still his shaking hands. The money bag sat next to him in the passenger seat like a limp, sleeping dog.

He grabbed the bag and stepped out of the car, making sure he slammed the door. He hoped Harper heard it. He didn't want to do this alone, not now, not ever.

Across the bridge, both doors of the car opened. A black guy—he recognized him as the guy he shot—stepped out of the driver's side, wearing jeans, high-tops, and a Memphis Redbirds jersey. A pistol filled his right hand. From the passenger side, a tall white man stepped out. In a suit and tie, of all things. His white shirt practically glowed in the dark. He looked like a businessman or a maybe even a preacher—calm, clean-shaven face, hair cut short. A look of serene confidence that he found totally unnerving. He appeared unarmed, and his hands rested at his sides.

He stopped at the edge of the bridge. He waited, unsure of the protocol. He hoped like hell Harper and that big-ass deputy were behind him.

"You Hack?" he called across the twenty yards of concrete that separated the two cars.

The black guy eased behind the open driver's side door. The white guy smiled.

"You may call me that, yes," the white guy said. "And you are Delmer Blackburn, thief and murderer."

He nodded his head toward the driver. "How do I know he won't kill me?"

"Because that's my job," Hack said. Still calm. Never raised his voice. "I presume that bag in your hand contains the money you stole from my employer."

"Yeah, I got your money, but not until you tell me our deal is still on."

"You are not in a position to interrogate or negotiate, Delmer. But I can assure you that the terms upon which we agreed are still valid."

"Whatever," he said. "Long as we got a deal." He noticed Hack was no longer paying attention. His face now glared at him, no, past him, his eyes shining like a predatory animal.

He was about to turn around when he heard it: footsteps behind him.

COLT

"Let's go," he said, stepping out of the truck into the suffocating humid night air. He clicked the door shut and waited as John climbed out. He stepped up the shoulder onto the dirt road.

"Damn, it's still hot," John said. "I'll never get used to this shit."

He smiled, then stepped toward the scene on the bridge, which was illuminated by butterscotch halos of parking lights. He saw, and heard, Delmer talking to two men.

"Hear that?" John said.

"Yep."

"That kid is sounding way too jumpy."

"Yep. We need to move."

They strode abreast through the darkness. Old, nearly forgotten sensations crept into his body and mind, and he knew John felt it, too.

They got to the bridge as Delmer trembled and swore under his breath after Hack told him something about a deal.

So, Delmer, you little shit, you think you got all your bases covered tonight.

He unsnapped his holster and kept his hand on his pistol. The car on the far side faced away, both doors open, a young black man behind the driver's door and a tall man in a suit in front of the passenger door—Hack, in a different, but no less expensive, suit.

"John," he said.

"Got it." John moved off to his left, closer to Delmer.

Hack and the other man saw the movement and peered at them. He stepped onto the bridge and nodded at Delmer. "Evening, Delmer," he said.

The kid looked stricken. "Uh, evening, Sheriff," was all he could manage.

He pointed at the driver. "You," he said, "I can't place, but you"—he swiveled his head and pointed at Hack—"I've met. I believe you introduced yourself to me as Hack."

Hack looked at him with unabashed curiosity, as if he were unaccustomed to being addressed so directly.

"You are correct, Sheriff Harper," Hack said. "You will, of course, excuse my speechlessness at your unexpected appearance."

The black kid snapped his head toward Hack. "That's Harper?" he said. "The fuck is he doing here?"

"Close your mouth, Dee," Hack said.

"You don't sound speechless to me," he said to Hack. "It seems you are still after something of great value to you. Is that how you put it? I'm going to guess that would be that bag of money Delmer has with him. But that money's not going anywhere."

Hack shifted his weight.

"Keep your hands where I can see 'em," he said. The black kid focused his attention on Delmer, and he realized the black kid must be the guy Delmer wounded.

"I also understand you been asking a lot of questions about me," he said, still talking to Hack. "Now we don't know each other all that well, so what seems to be the problem?

"Sheriff, allow me to be brief, seeing as you interrupted a business transaction," Hack said. "The problem, as you call it, is that my employer places a certain value on his employees who provide certain services. If that employee is no longer available, it costs my employer money, in terms of both revenue lost and overhead to replace him. You made one of those employees unavailable. My employer decided that you should bear at least part of that cost, and he sent me to see that cost passed on to you."

He couldn't believe this guy. "Jesus," he said. "You always talk like this? That's a shitload of words to say you aim to kill me for shooting that dirtbag Kenny Jenkins."

"If you prefer, then," Hack said. "Yes."

From the corner of his eye, he could see that John had moved to the side of Delmer, who seemed to be coming apart at the seams. He was practically quaking, from fear or rage, he couldn't tell. John, on the other hand, was ready, cool, and alert.

"I don't think so," he said. "I think you have costs of your own coming. For the murders of Robert Pritchard and Rick Munny."

Hack smiled. "Based on what? The word of that little thief on the end? I'm afraid that won't hold up. You can arrest me, but you know I'll be out of a jail cell before you can lock the door."

"I didn't come out here to arrest you."

Hack's eyes widened at that, and his smile dropped a tiny bit. "You draw a hard line, Sheriff. And you are as I suspected," he said.

"How's that?"

Hack resumed his smile. "You enforce your own moral code rather than the one you were elected to enforce."

"I do my job," he said. "At least I have a moral code."

"Ah, but your insinuation is flawed," Hack said. He still stood, hands at his sides, as if he had all the time in the world. "I, in fact, do have a moral code, and I make no excuses for it. Nor do I try to hide behind the supposed nobility of the law. As alike as you and I are, on that point, we differ."

"I'm nothing like you," he said. He was growing tired of the conversation. Hack continued to smile at him.

"Do you really believe that, Sheriff?" Hack said. "Do you not see that the only difference between you and me is that badge you wear? That even though your entire purpose for being in your position is to uphold and enforce the law, you operate outside the law whenever it is convenient for you or suits your own purposes?"

From the corner of his eye, he caught movement to his left. Delmer took a step toward Hack's car. The black guy leveled a pistol in his direction, and all hell broke loose.

The black kid fired three rounds. Delmer screamed and doubled over, then collapsed face-first on the bridge span.

John moved like a cat, in a crouch, toward Delmer, firing as he went. Bullets tore into the car and ricochets howled off into the night. The black kid continued to fire from behind the car door.

He pulled and fired at the door himself, but shattered the window instead. He swung his aim back toward Hack, but the man had dived into the car, yelling at the kid.

He started moving left, toward John and Delmer—John crouched in a pool of blood collecting around them. Delmer lay prone and trembling, his head down on the bridge boards, moaning and blubbering.

He heard the car engine turn over and jerked his head toward the sound. The engine roared and smoked, and the car shot off into the blackness like it had been launched from an aircraft carrier. He spun and fired three shots, blowing out a taillight but not slowing the car one iota.

He scrambled to John, who had rolled Delmer over and now cradled his head in his lap. A bullet hole in his belly, just below his sternum, poured a steady flow of blood on the boards of the bridge, even as John tried to stanch it with his hand. Both Delmer and John were drenched in blood.

"John?" he said as he knelt.

"It's bad."

Delmer's face contorted in pain. "I knew this would happen," he said.

John gave him a look, and he returned it. John was right—it was bad. Delmer was close to bleeding out.

"Delmer," he said. "Get your shit together. We're going to get you to a hospital."

Delmer's body convulsed, and his head rolled back and forth.

"OK," he said. "Let's roll. Come on, John, let's get him in his car."

John nodded. "Right."

They carried Delmer, who was out of his head from the pain and slippery as a fish from the blood, and loaded him into the backseat of his car.

"Take him to the ER now," he said to John.

"Me? What the hell are you going to do?"

"I'm going to go find that chatty fucker."

John's eyes narrowed, and he started to say something.

"Go," he said.

John started the car, put it in gear, turned around, and sped off.

He ran to his truck. It was a long shot, he knew, but he wasn't giving up that easy. He floored it across the bridge and back to the highway, seeing nothing but darkness and vague shapes. He gunned the engine, pushing his speed as much as he dared on the narrow two-lane highway. After twenty minutes of futility, he backed off the accelerator, turned the truck around, and headed back toward the bridge.

Goddammit. you're not getting away from me, you son of a bitch. I'll find your ass and put a fucking bullet in your head. Which is what I should have done as soon as you started running your mouth with all your stupid moral code bullshit.

I should have done it. Why didn't I? Because I got a little carried away with myself. Face it, Harper, you wanted him to piss you off so you could have a reason. But he didn't. And you got so involved with that, you let that kid shoot somebody you were supposed to be protecting.

His cell chimed, startling him and breaking his train of thought. He pulled the phone from his shirt pocket and saw that it was John calling.

"Yeah, John, how's Delmer? Y'all made it to the hospital?"

"Just got to the ER. Colt, he didn't make it," John said. "Doctor said he lost too much blood before he got here."

He gripped the wheel and gritted his teeth. *This one is all on me.*

"Colt, did you hear me?"

He blew out a breath. "Yeah, John, I heard you. I'll be there directly."

"Yeah." John's voice sounded as if it was floating across a chasm, faint and light.

"I'll be there as soon as I can." He threw the phone to the seat.

Oh, this fucker is going to pay.

He pulled to the shoulder, slammed on his brakes, and he felt the truck fishtail in the loose gravel. He threw the gearshift into park and bailed out, then reached behind the seat for a hickory ax handle he'd had for as long as he could remember.

He stepped across the highway and climbed a low dirt embankment to a stand of pines, none bigger around than his leg. He slid his hands up and down the ax handle, feeling the gouges caused from years of use. He picked one tree at random and swung. The blow rattled his teeth and made his hands hurt. He grunted and swung again, sending bark flying. He could smell sap seeping from the gash he'd opened up in the flesh of the tree, and he cursed the night air as he bashed it with a violent rhythm that fed on itself. His mind clouded, and he felt as if he were bludgeoning himself, thrashing away years of practiced indifference to a world he cared as little for as it did for him, a flimsy armor of insouciance he'd encased himself in for as long as he could remember to insulate himself from the very darkness he felt closing on him right now, the darkness that wanted to take his very mind and soul. He battered the memories—and the faces—the darkness brought him: his father, the men he'd killed. And the years of the impotent rage that not even the justification of a badge could assuage. His breath came in ragged gasps, and sweat flew from his arms and face.

He ceased his assault and staggered back, nearly losing his balance and tumbling backward down the embankment. His hands throbbed and his lungs felt seared. The ax handle was slippery with sweat. The blond wood of the tree, exposed and shattered like bone, gleamed against the darkness and oozed sap in thick globules that shined in the moonlight.

He took a step back as—unbidden and at the vortex of the chaos of his mind—his mother's voice came to him again, singing of divine joy and blessed peace in her hymn as she stood in the cemetery. He gulped the hot night air, and shook his head, tried to rid his mind of the music, but again he heard her voice, clear and strong and beckoning him to an eternal refuge.

His shoulders sagged, and he calmed himself. He swiped his face with his forearm and turned, crossed the road, and climbed into his truck. His anger would not be wasted. He was angry at the right man at the right time and in the right manner.

HACK

The pistol tucked under his left armpit was a temptation as strong as lust, but he stilled the urge to wrap his hand around it and point it at Dee's head. He would not kill the boy, much as he wanted to right at this moment. At least not tonight. Not until Dee made up for his childish action.

"You were stupid," he said. "I can tolerate certain personality defects. Inexperience, slow-mindedness, even repressed anger—the latter of which you clearly possess. But I cannot, and will not, tolerate stupidity. Do you understand what I'm saying?"

Dee kept his eyes on the road and twisted his hands around the steering wheel, making squeaking sounds that competed with the thumping of the tires on the cracked asphalt.

"Yeah, I understand," he said. "As long as what I understand isn't that I'm about to get my eyes shot out."

"Which is exactly what you deserve."

Dee didn't answer; he concentrated on the highway ahead of him, checking his rearview as if Satan was chasing him.

He turned his mind to his next step, which he realized was the same as his original step—get the money back from Delmer Blackburn. Even so, he could hardly believe his good fortune at Colt Harper showing up on that bridge, though he now knew that Harper had been in control of that situation, not he, and that realization angered him further. He should have paid more attention to that. He underestimated Harper. At this point, however, it mattered little.

He placed his hands on his thighs to deny his temptations and thought more of his next move. He smiled—fortune was with him. He had another option, one that he was sure a man like Harper would be unable to let go unanswered.

"The woman," he said to Dee. "What is her name?"

"Woman? Oh, you mean that one I had to go look up? Rhonda Raines."

"That's right." He would use this woman, let her bring Harper to him. Properly motivated, she would do exactly as ordered.

He needed to plan this, and he needed reinforcement. He turned to Dee.

"Return to the house," he said.

Dee sighed and draped a wrist over the wheel, slouching into the drive.

They rode in silence for several miles, the humming of the tires punctuated only by the staccato of insects smashing into the windshield.

As Dee made the last right-hand turn onto the road leading to the house, the cell phone in his left jacket pocket vibrated—his personal cell, not the burner he used for business. He pulled it out and recognized the number. He frowned and noted the time.

"Hello, Mr. Brooks," he said as he raised the phone to his ear.

"I don't customarily make calls at this hour," Brooks said, his words like darts in his ears. "But seeing as I've heard nothing to indicate that you've done the job you were hired to do, I'm calling to ask you just what in the hell I'm paying you for."

He stared at the roof of the car, clicked his teeth. Drew a breath, let out half.

"You're paying me to recover that which was taken from you and to take care of one other nettlesome entity."

"Hack, I never know what the fuck you're saying."

"I'm working on it."

"You're *working* on it? What the hell does *that* mean?"

"It means that both of your problems are about to be solved, probably at the same time. Within forty-eight hours by my estimate. And that's all I care to say over a cell phone."

Silence. Then a cough. "Dammit, Hack, this better get done, and it better get done fast."

"Or what?"

"Don't push me. Or you'll find out." Brooks broke the connection.

He put the phone away. He looked forward to doing just that. But first things first.

Dee glanced over at him with renewed interest. "So," he said, "it's on, then? You really going after that sheriff?"

"I've been after him, as you put it, since the first time his name came up. The neutralization of this particular sheriff has always been my higher goal."

Dee smirked. "Seriously? I thought you was down here to teach them stupid dealers a lesson. Why's this guy so important to you? I mean, other than the fact that he shot one of your boss's dudes a while back? That ain't no skin off you, right?"

He looked at Dee. "The elimination of Sheriff Harper will ensure the restoration of my status with Mr. Brooks. My redemption, if you will."

"Redemption? Shit, man, that's heavy," Dee said. "That redemption shit could also bring down a ton of heat on you and your boss. Naw, you got some other reason for that, right?"

He turned the air conditioner up a notch. "Not that I owe you or anyone else an explanation, but Harper is an obstacle. An impediment to the furtherance of commerce in this area. And he will not be intimidated or persuaded to move aside. And nobody stands in my way. No one. Ergo, he must be eliminated."

Dee nodded, his face solemn. He gave him one furtive glance, then steered the car into the gravel driveway and cut the ignition.

"And when that commerce expands, you get all the credit," Dee said.

He popped open his door. "Yes, something like that."

MOLLY

S he had to admit, she had a fondness for the free breakfast buffets offered in most hotels these days. Certainly wasn't something she'd admit to around her mother, but, then, her mother didn't necessarily need to know.

The waffle iron dinged, and she flipped the handle and knocked the waffle onto her Styrofoam plate with a plastic fork, then grabbed two packages of syrup from the basket and made her way to a table by the faux fireplace. She drank from the coffee cup she'd brought down from her room and shook her head in an attempt to wake herself fully. She'd grabbed a local paper from the front desk, spread it out, and scanned the front page as she prepared to eat. The top story this morning concerned the arrest of a man accused of beating his parents over a fast-food order.

She contemplated going back upstairs and crawling back into bed. Her "vacation" had begun to feel more like what it really was—a self-imposed exile. She'd come up empty at every turn, and had little motivation to keep going. She knew she would eventually, just not today.

She ate slowly, reading the paper as the TV above the fireplace droned—a local morning news show. She neared the end of the fast-food assault story, then heard the anchor's voice enunciating "gunshot wound." Her head snapped up, and she stared at the anchor, a very young black man in a blue suit, who was describing an incident from the night before.

"Authorities tell us the bridge was the scene of the shooting," he said as B-roll appeared over his shoulder—an old, low metal bridge that reached over a small, sluggish-looking brown creek. At both ends of the span sat law enforcement vehicles. Uniformed deputies and state troopers milled about on the bridge, and small orange cones were set at random places, several near a dark spot on the weathered and bowed planks running the length of the bridge. She presumed that spot to be a bloodstain.

"Passersby on nearby Highway 45 said they saw several odd flashes, in the words of one driver, and the police department received three calls reporting it. But because the bridge is in rural part of the county and rarely used anymore, there were no eye-witnesses. One driver, though, heard a series of gunshots between ten p.m. and midnight last night, but it was too hard to tell where the shots were coming from," the anchorman said. "The Baptist Memorial emergency room reported treating a white man in his thirties for a gunshot wound to the abdomen. The man, whose name is being withheld pending notification of next of kin, died about half an hour after his arrival, at eleven thirty-two p.m. The sheriff's department declined to discuss the case in any detail, citing an ongoing investigation."

She dropped her fork into her syrup-covered waffle. *A midnight shootout on a bridge. Holy shit.*

It was her guy. Had to be. She scooped up the remains of her breakfast, shoved it into a trash can, and headed to the front desk.

The young woman behind the desk looked worn out from her overnight shift, but managed a smile. "Can I help you, ma'am?" she asked.

She smiled back. "Checking out. And can you tell me how to get to the Baptist Memorial Hospital?"

An hour later, she pulled up at the entrance of the emergency room. She pulled her hair into a ponytail, then climbed out of her car. She didn't look much like a federal agent, in jeans, T-shirt, and hiking boots, but she had her gun and her badge, and that would have to do at the moment.

Inside, the ER was as quiet as a morgue. *Definitely not Memphis*, she thought as she approached the check-in desk. A small, mousy woman in purple scrubs decorated with pink ponies saw her and peered at her from under her eyebrows. "Help you, ma'am?"

She smiled. "I'm looking for anyone on the staff who attended the shooting victim last night."

The woman, who looked to be in her forties and sounded as if Marlboro Reds were her brand, didn't change her expression or move. Her hands remained on her keyboard. "And you are?" she said.

"Oh, sorry." She fished her badge case from her back pocket. "Special Agent Molly McDonough, Bureau of Alcohol, Tobacco, Firearms, and Explosives." She held the badge against the Plexiglas.

The woman's eyes scanned her ID, her still-neutral expression becoming an annoyance.

"Wait here," the woman said, finally moving. She stood and left through a door at the rear of her office.

She surveyed the unremarkable waiting room. Three people sat in low plastic chairs, nowhere near each other. One flipped through a *National Geographic* while the other two watched the news on the flat-screen TV mounted high on the wall to her right. The subtitles informed her of a plane crash near Birmingham, a two-seat single-engine private aircraft. Pilot killed.

"Ma'am?"

She turned to face the Woman with the Marlboro Voice standing next to a fit, bespectacled thirtyish man in the white overcoat and stethoscope of a doctor.

"Dr. Bateman can help you," Marlboro Voice said.

"Thank you," she said and smiled. She extended her hand and introduced herself.

"Harold," Dr. Bateman said. "Let's step back here to my office."

After he closed the door in the closet he called an office, she flashed her badge, and they sat at the doctor's desk while she told him what she'd heard and seen on the TV news. He nodded throughout, his face attentive.

"Yes, he'd been shot in the abdomen by a nine-millimeter weapon, most likely a handgun," Bateman said. "He'd lost a lot of blood before he even got here. I thought we'd be able to stabilize him, but we weren't able to. Too much blood loss. He died in the OR."

"The news said his name was being withheld."

Bateman nodded. "Yeah, that's up to the police, as you know."

"True," she said. "But can I get it from you?"

For the first time, Bateman looked puzzled. "Excuse me, but I have to ask what this is in connection with? I don't doubt your credentials, but this is highly unusual."

She smiled. "Certainly, Doctor. I'm investigating, have been for a while, a series of murders that I believe are connected. Perpetrated by the man who shot your victim. He likes to shoot people at close range."

Bateman nodded, apparently satisfied. He reached into a stack of file folders on his desk and pulled a slim one onto a marked-up coffee-stained desktop calendar.

"The victim was Delmer Blackburn," he said, reading from the folder. "Mississippi driver's license. Columbus address."

"Who brought him in?"

The doctor leaned back in his chair. "Deputy sheriff, but he wasn't in uniform. Musclebound black guy, probably in his midforties. Very short hair, wearing a gun, which I chewed his ass about."

"I'm wearing a gun."

"We're not in the ER trying to save a man's life," Bateman said. "Ma'am."

"He say how it happened?"

Bateman looked skeptical. "Yeah, he said it was a drug deal gone bad, and that's all I needed to know."

"You got a name on this deputy?"

"Sure," Bateman said and opened a desk drawer. Pulled out a thin hanging folder. "John Carver. He introduced himself when the sheriff showed up."

"I'm sorry," she said. "I'm confused. The sheriff?"

Bateman frowned, puzzled. "Yeah, Sheriff Harper came in a few minutes later. The victim had already expired, actually."

"And what did he say?"

"Same thing as the deputy. The deceased had been engaged in an illegal drug transaction and had gotten shot, that it was under investigation, and that he'd have to notify the next of kin."

"I see. You said the deputy was not in uniform. What about the sheriff?"

The doctor snorted. "You're not from around here, are you? Sheriff Harper hardly ever wears a uniform, unless you call a badge and a gun and an attitude like one of them ol'-timey Texas Rangers without the hat a uniform."

"Anything strike you as unusual about this incident?"

"No, other than the fact that the deputy had a lot of blood on his clothes, and Harper had a look in his eyes."

"A look?"

"A look like he didn't want to be trifled with. But neither did I. I'd just had a patient bleed out in the other room. He told me the circumstances were none of my business."

She put her notebook away. "Thank you for time, Dr. Bateman."

"Happy to help."

COLT

He took a beer from Delmer's refrigerator and opened on it on the back porch. Sat on the wooden steps leading to the overgrown grass and drank it half down.

The screen door groaned behind him, and he knew it was John without having to look. He and John could have entire conversations without having to talk, but he knew that this was not one of those occasions.

John had his own beer, the bottle sweating in his hand. He stepped off the back porch into the dazzling, relentless sun and stared at the unruly yard. He raised his bottle and took a long pull.

"You know," John said. "This shit ain't your fault."

He squinted at John's back and took a drink. "Easy for you to say."

John kept staring across the yard into a stand of trees about forty yards distant. "The hell it is. I was there, remember? You had no way of knowing how that was going to go down."

"Yeah, well. You know sometimes shit goes sideways in ways you could never guess. And I hope to God you didn't come out to give me the 'I told you so' treatment."

"No," John said, "I didn't. But I do think this guy is trouble. "He ain't no redneck drunk. And he wasn't scared of you at all. He had that stone-cold killer feel about him."

"I noticed. I also noticed had he tried to pull on me I'da dropped him like a rock."

"Yeah, well, we'll have to wait and see on that, thanks to that little banger he had with him."

His phone buzzed in his pocket. He wanted to ignore it because it was only a matter of time before the local press put two and two together and came looking.

He didn't recognize the number, but the area code—9-0-1— was Memphis. He didn't know anybody in Memphis. Hadn't been there in years.

"Harper."

"Excuse me, did you say Harper?" Woman's voice. He shot John a "What the fuck?" look.

"I did. Who's this?"

"You first."

"Ma'am, I don't have time for this."

"Oh, you've got time, Sheriff Harper." This broad, whoever she was, had an attitude. "You've got time to explain to me how you were involved in a shooting on a bridge last night."

He stood, dusted the seat of his pants. John followed him up and stood like a totem next to him.

"Are you a reporter?"

"No, I'm Special Agent Molly McDonough of the Bureau of Alcohol, Tobacco, Firearms, and Explosives. And you still haven't answered my question."

He squinted his eyes shut and sighed. He looked at John and mouthed, "A-T-F." John mouthed back, "Fuck."

"Well, Special Agent McDonough, you know all I got to do is hang up."

"Go ahead. I'll meet you at your office?"

He shook his head and stared off into the glare, thinking of chaos and butterflies.

"What do you want?"

"For starters, an explanation of what happened last night."

"That's a local matter, Agent McDonough. No need for the feds to be involved."

Silence. That got her stumped.

"Sheriff, we need to talk," McDonough said.

"Where are you?"

"Standing on the bridge where Delmer Blackburn got shot. You remember that bridge, right?"

For fuck's sake.

John was already shaking his head. He shrugged. Looked at his watch.

"Meet me at Sam's Smokehouse in an hour."

"OK, where is it?"

"From where you are, get back on 45 North and stay on it through town. Go past the turnoff for the air force base. You'll see it."

She said something, but he didn't hear it as he broke the connection. John crossed his arms. "Dammit, Colt," he said. "What does that agent want?"

"I'm going to find out."

"You want me to come with you?"

"No, I got this one."

A half hour later, he wheeled into the nearly deserted parking lot that clung to the highway and parked near the front door of Sam's.

Inside the place reminded him of a barn, with one central rough-hewn room and some sort of crazy-quilt plywood construction—walls, counters, ceiling, all a wild pattern of raw plywood.

He walked past several wooden tables covered in pink plastic sheets to the long counter festooned with Coke ads. The aroma of barbecue seemed to emanate from behind the counter that ran the width of the room and the tan, busty woman in a red tank top behind the register. Her wild brown hair, no doubt frizzed out by the humidity, was bunched up on top of her head and held in place with a bright red hairband. She smiled as she spoke into the phone held between her ear and a hunched shoulder. She saw him walk up and nodded. He nodded back and let her finish.

Overhead, a ceiling fan worked overtime at cooling the cavernous room and blowing the barbecue smell over the half dozen diners at various tables. Fluorescent lights hummed, even with plenty of sunlight coming in from the bank of windows on the front wall of the dining room.

"Sorry to keep you waiting, hon," the register woman said as she set down the phone.

He smiled and ordered a plate of ribs, grabbed a beer from the cooler to the right of the register, and took a seat near the wall facing the door. To his right, a couple—sixties, married, most likely—chewed silently without giving him a second glance.

The register woman came to his table all smiles and damp hair and cleavage, carrying his plate. "Here you go, hon," she said, huffing a wisp of hair from her face. "Anything else I can get you?"

He smiled up at her, saw the look in her eyes, and shook his head. "No, thank you. I think I'm good."

"Mmmhmmm," she said. "Well, if you need something, give me a holler."

"Will do," he said to her already twitching behind as she retreated to the counter.

He was halfway through his ribs when she walked in. And she didn't look much like a federal agent: not very tall, dark-red ponytail, jeans, oversized blue T-shirt—probably hiding a sidearm—and hiking boots. G-Shock watch. Fit, probably a runner.

She saw him at the same time and nodded. She looked as if she were giving him a similar appraisal. It was a unique and curious sensation.

She walked straight to him, green eyes boring into his own. She stopped behind the chair opposite him and slid her hands into her pockets. Up close, he could see she was far more attractive than he'd thought.

"Sheriff Harper?" she asked, her voice low. He grabbed a paper napkin from the dispenser and nodded.

"I am," he said and nodded at the chair. "Have a seat. Unless you're going to order something to eat. I can recommend the ribs."

She cocked her head toward the counter. The busty woman stared back at her. "I do like ribs," she said. She walked to the counter, placed an order, then sat across from him with her own bottle of beer. She slid a flat leather case across the table. He lifted one corner, saw the gold badge, slid it back.

"OK," he said. "You're bona fide." He reached into his back pocket and slid his own badge case toward her. She mimicked his inspection and nodded.

"So are you," she said.

He pocketed the badge and took a pull from his longneck. "So what brings you to Mississippi, Special Agent McDonough? All the way from Memphis, I presume."

She drank from her own bottle, made a face. "Boy, that's good," she said. The waitress arrived, put her plate in front of her and left without a word. If McDonough noticed the snub, she didn't let on. She waited a beat, then said, "Let's say I'm on vacation."

He laughed. "Vacation? You always carry a gun when you're on vacation?"

"Do you?" Her eyebrows rose. "I'm not much for cute little conversations, especially when we both know it's bullshit."

He grinned. "Do tell. Then get to it."

"I know your deputy brought Delmer Blackburn to the ER last night, and he was gutshot. And you showed up shortly after, and told the doctor he'd been in some kind of illegal drug activity. I have a feeling you were there when Blackburn got shot, which makes you at the very least a material witness to a homicide, if not a suspect. At least at this point—especially since your behavior at the ER could be called shady."

He sat back in his chair. OK, she was smart. Hard-nosed. But what the fuck was she doing here? "Suspect?" he said. "Seriously? And where do you get off calling me shady when I was doing my job as the duly elected sheriff of this county? You're a little far from Memphis, aren't you? As in, out of your jurisdiction."

She leaned toward him, elbows also on the table, green eyes flashing. To the other tables, they could have been a couple having a fight. "I am a federal agent. My jurisdiction is everywhere. Look, I know you didn't kill Blackburn, but I called you a suspect just because you're belligerent. I think the guy who killed him has been executing drug dealers—low-level ones—in this area, probably hired by someone to punish them and send a message. And he might be a serial killer. I think I can connect him to the death of a woman in Knoxville."

She took a bite of the ribs on her plate and chewed. Clearly, she enjoyed them.

"Then why haven't you? Connected him, I mean," he said. "And why just you? Where's your big ol' team of feds and SUVs?"

He watched her expression flicker, just a heartbeat, from neutral to angry and back again, and it dawned on him.

"Oh," he said. "There is no case. You're out here snooping around on your own. Probably without authority. Nice. And you have the audacity to call *me* shady."

She jabbed a finger at him, and he raised his eyebrows in surprise, a move that angered her even more.

"Knock it off, Sheriff, before I run your ass—" She caught herself and settled back into her seat. Took a pull off her beer. Blew out a breath. Then she smiled. "I'm on vacation, like I said. And I happened to hear about this shooting."

He smiled back. "Bullshit. Let me guess. You have a hunch about a killer. A hunch not shared by your higher-ups, who told you to go pound sand. You said fuck that and started following this hunch anyway."

She nodded. "Something like that," she said through a mouthful of pork.

"I thought rogue agents were only in the movies."

"They are. I'm officially on leave. That's the truth. What I do on my own time is my business."

"In my county, that means your business is my business."

Anger again. "What are you after here, Sheriff? Reelection? This is the third killing in just a few weeks. You haven't caught the guy. Why not put the word out far and wide and cast a net for this guy?"

He thought about that question. "Like I said, it's a local matter."

She nearly choked on her food. "Local? Or personal?"

He crossed his arms. Her impertinence was getting on his nerves. "Look, unless you have some real reason to be here, I suggest you leave this matter to local law enforcement, which in this case is me, and continue your vacation somewhere else, like outside of my county."

She leaned back and sighed. "Look, you can sit there with your good-looking smile and all your redneck charm and try to bullshit me, but it's not going to work. You think you're the first guy to try that?"

He shifted in his seat and sipped his beer.

"Right," she said. "You're not. Hell, you're not even the first one from Mississippi to try it."

That intrigued him, and he couldn't keep a smile from crawling across his face.

"None of your business," she said, reading his mind. "And not the point. The point is there's a man killing people out there, and I think you and I are after the same person. Seems to me we can double the chances of arresting this guy, and everybody wins."

He looked at her hard for a second, then figured what the hell. "When I find this guy, I'm going to kill him."

"Not if I have anything to do with it. And before you start to tell me that's not how y'all do things down here, I'll remind you that this man is likely responsible for more murders than what he's already apparently committed. So don't think you can go all vigilante on me. He's going to be arrested and tried in a court of law."

"Really?" he said. "You ever had a man try to kill you, Agent McDonough?"

MOLLY

The question hit her like an accusation. One she'd been ready to answer for years.

"Yes, I have, Sheriff Harper," she said, looking him in the eyes. "A man named Rodney Spears. Shot him dead on a beach in Hawaii. Had no choice. One in the head, one in the chest, just like I was trained to do."

His face changed. Not the insouciant, in-control lawman now. She could tell he was reappraising her and, if she had to bet, liked what he saw in her as a law enforcement professional.

"Yeah," she said. "A few years ago. I was still new, working in DC when some rifles went missing from an armory at the Marine Corps base on Oahu. Long story, but I got sent there by the assistant director of the bureau to get a handle on the situation."

"Why you?" Harper asked. "Sorry, what I mean is, why not the local office?"

She shrugged. "Like I said, long story. Back then, I kinda had a rep as a hard charger after cracking a case on a serial bomber in Memphis. So I got sent. There was a small group of locals on Oahu who were basically a domestic terrorist group. Had this idea of forcing the United States to let Hawaii form its own government. Nuts. But nuts who had managed to steal rifles, kill a guy, and steal a Stinger missile from a navy ship. And planned to shoot down a seven forty-seven over Honolulu."

"Shit," Harper said. "Why did I never hear anything about this?"

"Because the way we were able to stop them was on account of a former agent who lived there, and he was the one who discovered all this. He was a pariah, hardheaded, and fucking brilliant. He figured it all out, and we ended up chasing two guys down a beach at night. We stopped them just as they were setting up. Rodney Spears drew a weapon on me, and I shot him."

"So?"

"So, what?"

"Nobody even heard about this?" Harper said.

"Nope," she said. "The whole thing embarrassed the hell out of ATF. And I got buried. I was sent out there to prevent a former, persona non grata agent—who *was* kinda going rogue, actually—from doing anything, and I ended up working with him. So I was reprimanded for disobeying a direct order, bringing discredit, blah, blah, blah."

"That's bullshit. You saved a lot of lives."

"Yeah, it was bullshit," she said, unable to stop talking. "But it was not long after 9/11 and nobody wanted that kind of shit in the press. So I got exiled back to Memphis."

Harper stared at her, nodded. "I'm sorry," he said.

She took a long pull off her beer and looked away. The room felt hot and uncomfortable all of a sudden.

Harper kept staring at her. "So this is your chance at redemption."

She started at that. He was a quick study, this one. She nodded slowly and looked across the table at him. "Yes, it is."

COLT

"**H**is name is Hackett," he said. "Lewis Hackett. He didn't shoot Delmer Blackburn—that was some gangbanger-looking kid with him."

He told her what happened on the bridge, and he noticed that even though she took no notes, she took in every word. She was smart and a pro. And possibly doomed.

He finished his lunch while she walked him through her one-person investigation, and he had to admit she was thorough and intuitive. Her hunches made sense. There was a lot of talk about databases and analysis and macros that he didn't understand, but he got the gist of it. And it sure as hell sounded like the same guy. He said so as he wiped the barbecue sauce off his hands.

"So," she said, pushing her own plate to the side. "How do we get this guy?"

"Give him his money."

She squinted, her face a question.

"We still have the money Delmer was supposed to give him on the bridge," he said. "He'll still be wanting that. And me."

"You?"

"Yeah, me. I have my own long story, but the short of it is, this guy isn't just after the money. He's out to bring my head on a plate back to his boss in Memphis."

She furrowed her brow. "For?"

"I shot one of his guys a while back. Local dumbass. But this Hack person thinks he can score some points by whacking me."

That surprised her, he could tell. He rose, and she followed suit. "I'm going to talk to John, my deputy, see if we can set up a money meeting," he said. "When I do, I'll call you."

"You better," she said.

JOHN

"Thanks," he said as Rhonda refilled his mug with coffee. He'd been there half an hour, sitting at her kitchen table at the end of a workday. Under normal circumstances, he enjoyed the time luxuriating in her company, conversation, and laughter. It had become a very pleasant habit. Except for the discussion of some of the details of his job, which he had just spent the last ten minutes doing. But today he wondered if this would be the last time he would get this opportunity. He had seen Hack up close, and, though he wouldn't admit it to Colt, the guy caused him to feel fear for the first time in a long time.

"He's taking this very personally," he said. "It's like this guy, I don't know, stirs up something in Colt that sets him off. When we were on the bridge, I watched him change from, you know, a sheriff—a cop—into something out of an old western. He practically dared the guy to pull on us."

Rhonda looked back at him. "He does have a way of taunting you."

He nodded. "Yeah, but it was more than that. He used a phrase one time—when I got shot. 'Old anger,' he called it. He had a look on his face like he was a thousand miles away."

She tucked the carafe back into the machine and sat across the table from him with her own cup. "Honestly, John, I never have understood how y'all do what you do. Scares me to death to even think about that. "Losing you. Losing Colt. Either of you."

Her words landed on him wrong, especially after the conversation he'd had with Colt. Seemed like every conversation had to include Colt's name. "I know it's scary Rhonda, but me and Colt know how to handle it."

She nodded, looked down at the coffee steaming in her cup. "I know y'all do but that's not much comfort when you're out there handling it. I can't lose anything else, John. Not after Clifford."

"I'm not going to do anything reckless."

A smile flashed, then disappeared.

He blew across the top of his mug, took a sip. "But can I tell you something?"

She cocked her head at him, curious, maybe even startled. "Of course you can."

He cleared his throat. "I like you, Rhonda. A lot, you know that. I like what we have."

"But?"

"But sometimes it feels like I can never get Colt to leave the room."

Her brow furrowed, and she looked uncomfortable. "What do you mean?"

"Even now. You just said you can't lose him. Look, I know y'all have history. I get that. But sometimes I feel like I'm just standing in for him. Like some kind of, I don't know, pinch hitter."

Her expression told him he had just offended her, and he hated himself for even bringing up the subject.

"John," she said.

"I'm sorry. I shouldn't have brought it up."

Rhonda met his eyes. "John, listen to me," she said in a voice choked with memories. She smiled and looked away, and he saw her eyes mist for an instant, like she had just remembered someone lost a long time ago. "Colt was a sweet, gentle boy when we met. We were so young."

"Colt was sweet?"

"Mmmhmmm, very. But he was also confused, hurt, and very angry. His father's foolishness hurt him, but he has his own demons. I saw those demons get hold of him, right in front of my eyes, and I don't want to ever see that again. That old anger you're talking about. It changed the way I looked at Colt."

"How?"

She looked down at the table. "It was so long ago. Colt and I went out on a date, if you can believe that, when we were in high school. And you can probably guess that a white boy and a black girl on a date didn't happen too much around here back in those days."

He nodded, not knowing what to say.

She laced her fingers together in front of her and stared off into the distance, or into the past, it seemed. "We went all the way to Starkville just to watch a movie, in the hopes we wouldn't be seen by anyone who knew us." She laughed, a low bitter sound. "Turns out, it didn't matter."

"Somebody did see you?"

"Not anyone we knew. Three boys, white boys, harassed us on the way back to Colt's car, saying vile, hateful things. Colt made sure I got to the car safely, then he turned on them. It got ugly."

"Go on," he said.

She pressed her lips together and drew a ragged breath. "It was terrifying, John. Colt was getting beaten by these boys, but he managed to get the car door open, and he pulled out an ax handle—I have no idea where he got it—and he beat all three of those boys to a pulp. I mean, I thought he had killed them. You can imagine how scared I was. I think it scared him as much as me."

"Colt? Really?" He leaned back in his chair. "I had no idea. Never seen him scared. Not even in combat."

She rose and refilled their cups. "Yes, well, like I said, it changed the way I looked at him. We drove home and never spoke of it again. And that was the end of our romance." She smiled at the word, then looked directly at him. "So, no, John, you are not pinch-hitting for Colt, or for any man for that matter. I'm with you precisely because you aren't like him. Yes, you're both cops and Marine buddies and all that, but you have that gentleness that Colt no longer has. If he had it at all, it was before that night."

He nodded, trying to understand. "I see," he said, even though he wasn't sure if he really did.

She put her hand on his. "Let me put it to you this way," she said. "Colt has always had my back. When Clifford died, I knew Colt would find the man who did it. I believed it. And I even prayed that Colt would kill him. I really did. I've known that about him my whole life. And I've always known that he's there if I ever need that kind of...ferocity. But I could never be part of that—not in a relationship. I don't feel safe that way. He's very dear to me. But there's no denying he's a violent man. Some people can reconcile love and violence, or accommodate it. But I can't. You need to know that as much as I care for Colt, it is completely different from how I feel about you. I feel safe with you. Do you understand that?"

"I think so."

"Colt has always had my back," she said, as if she'd not heard anything he'd said. "And I love him for that."

He shrugged. "I love him like a brother, too."

COLT

He had to give it to her, she was fast and professional. If not a bit ambitious for his liking.

He sat across from Molly at Snider's, a tiny store near the state line on Old 82. Their table, one of only two in the joint, sat to one side of the store, near the deli counter, at the opposite end of the aisles of home goods and fishing tackle. The other table, occupied by a couple with a toddler, sat on the other side, near the canned goods aisle. The place reeked of cooking grease and the catfish plates they'd each demolished in the middle of the afternoon while the owner/cook/waiter watched them from the register. Over lunch, they'd pieced together a timeline of the murders, and he'd listened to more of McDonough's theories. She seemed to have a lot of them.

"Plus," she said, wiping her fingers with a paper napkin and moving the plastic basket to the side, "I was able to dig a little, now that I have a name."

He sipped iced tea. "We already ran him."

"Yeah, but you said his juvie record was sealed."

"Don't tell me you—"

"No," she said. "Sealed is sealed. She pulled a folder from the backpack at her feet and opened it on the table. "But I was able to pull up his name in some of our d-bases—that's one thing I'm damn good at."

"And?"

"He's been connected in one way or another to the Dixie Mafia, a bootlegging ring in Kentucky, and the Mexican cartels—or at least one of them."

"Doing what?"

"Hard to say. Usually, though, it looks like muscle."

"So, he's a well-dressed thug."

She cocked her head at him. "Huh?"

"When I met him, he was wearing an expensive suit. Didn't come across as some hillbilly thug."

"Oh." She sipped at her tea. "There's more. Seems that as a teenager, back in Kentucky, he was implicated in the rape and murder of a learning-disabled girl about the same age."

He whistled. "That explains the sealed record."

"Yeah," she said, "but if you dig deep enough you can still find stuff in newspapers. And this murder created quite the scandal in the holler."

"I'm sure."

"After the girl died, her father was shot to death in his front yard one night by an unknown assailant. Just happened to be the same day Hackett ran away from home, carrying nothing but his .410 shotgun."

"Let me guess."

"Yep. Girl's father—Reginald McCall—killed by a single shotgun blast. Apparently he accused Hackett publicly, confronted the elder Hackett at his home. A slight to hillbilly honor, that sort of thing."

Outside, he heard two car doors slam. "Anything else?"

"No, that's about it."

He glanced out the store window and froze. Hack and the black kid were walking toward the door.

"I'll be damned," he said.

"What?" McDonough said, then looked out the window. "Those two?" Then, "Oh, shit. That's Hack, isn't it?"

He looked across the table at her. She was still cool. "Yeah. Look, head over to one of those aisles where you have a clear line of sight."

She understood and was up and gone before he could turn his head back to the window. He grabbed her food basket and pulled it to his side of the table and moved her backpack behind his seat just as the door rattled and the little bell at the top tinkled. Hack strode in, the black kid limping behind him.

He pushed his chair back and watched them approach. Put his hand on his holster, popped the snap.

Hack, wearing another expensive suit without a tie, stopped about five feet short. Black kid to his left, hands on his hips.

"Mr. Hack," he said, not bothering with preamble. "I hope you're not stalking me. That would not be a healthy course of action."

Hack glared at him. No toothy smile today.

"Sheriff, you are still in possession of something of value to me."

"Delmer? Hell, you took care of him two nights ago. Or was that you?" He pointed to the kid.

Hack didn't answer.

"Oh," he said. "The money is what you want. Sorry. Impounded. You'll have to go back to your bosses empty-handed."

Now Hack smiled. "Perhaps not. As I alluded to the other night, my employer would pay a generous reward for your badge—dead, not alive."

"Do tell. You didn't fare so well on the bridge. You think you can do that today?"

"I believe the odds are in my favor today," Hack said. He tilted his head toward the black kid, who was doing his best to look tough.

He stood and stepped around the table, hand still on his pistol. "You sure about that?" he said, and cut his eyes toward Molly.

Hack, then the kid, turned to see her standing ten feet behind them, in front of a table where a family stared at this sudden confrontational scene. She stared at Hack with hard eyes and eased her hand to her hip, revealing the pistol under her shirt. He had to fight the urge to smile.

Hack faced him again, eyes blazing. "Some other time, Sheriff."

"Obviously, you know how to find me," he said. "But hear me on this, Hack. The next time you and I see each other, I won't be this talkative. Or accommodating."

Hack's lip curled in a sneer. "I look forward to it, Harper."

"Not as much as me."

Hack turned and stomped out of the store. The kid jumped, startled, and hobbled after him.

McDonough rushed to the table. "Jesus," she said. "Why in the hell didn't you arrest him?"

He nodded toward the other end of the store. The parents and toddler were as still and mute as the cans on the shelves behind them. "Civilians," he said.

Molly's eyes went wide, then her face darkened in a scowl. "You had me as backup," she said. "I could have covered him while you walked his ass outside."

"I didn't think of that at the time," he said, staring out the window.

"Well, what the fuck were you thinking?"

"That if I drew down on him with these civilians here, it would have been a bloodbath."

She put her hands on her hips, obviously furious. "So a murderer just walks out of here. That's pretty goddamn stupid."

"I'm beginning to think the same thing, now that we're having this conversation."

"I'll tell you what else is stupid," she said. "Getting off on this little Gary Cooper thing you got going."

He grimaced. "Yeah, maybe."

"Stupid and negligent."

"Shut up, McDonough."

"Hey, I'm not the one who let him walk," she said. She walked around him and snatched up her backpack. "Did you even get a look at the car or the plates?"

"Ford Taurus."

"Tennessee plates," she said. She put her hands on her hips. "Jesus, Harper."

"I said shut up," he said. "He'll be back. I have his money."

HACK

He fought his anger back into a box so that he could think clearly. His wrath was awakening and beginning to pace back and forth across his mind, demanding to be satiated. Soon, he told himself. Soon.

"Dee, I want you to contact Strickland, Foster, and Preston," he said as the kid wheeled the car back onto the highway, headed west on the two-lane road toward the orange late-afternoon sun. "Tell them their services are required at their usual fee, and they should leave Memphis for here immediately."

Dee cut his eyes at him. "You sure you want those guys?"

"I'm not asking for an opinion or an assessment."

"I understand that, but, seriously. I can see Strickland and Foster, even though those two rednecks don't have half a brain between them. But Preston is a fucking psycho."

"He is brutal and efficient and utterly unafflicted with squeamishness."

"Motherfucker medieval is what he is. Blowtorch a man's dick off. That's pretty fucked up."

"Shut up and drive, Dee. And bear in mind that the reason I'm giving this order is due to your recklessness at that bridge."

Dee sighed. He didn't say another word all the way back to Columbus.

When his anger had cooled, he looked at Dee. "Go to the house, then give me the keys."

Dee shrugged. "Whatever you want."

An hour later, he listened to the engine cool as he surveyed the downtown street. Even from a half a block away, he could tell what this was. AA meeting. Drunks and addicts were easy to spot, especially in broad daylight and near a church. The men leathery and skinny, with drawn faces and milky ratlike eyes. Twitchy from the detox and the nerve-jangling newness of being dried out and the panicky emotional rawness it caused. They had the faces of the craven, the hunted, the defeated yet defiant. Even the three men who smoked easily on the sidewalk near the entrance to the Baptist church, the ones who obviously had some semblance of recovery, they, too, had shadows behind their eyes, shadows caused by the demons of shame, sin, remorse, and the terrors of jail and the DTs.

He sat behind the wheel of his car, parallel parked on a downtown street facing the church with a clear view of the entrance to the small brick building behind the sanctuary of the church. He had been idle for twenty minutes.

The women were worse. They looked like a cross between electroshock treatment patients and horror movie wraiths, stringy and old before they'd had a chance to be young, bellies distended, jumpy like alley cats, shabby in disaster-relief clothing. Addiction was particularly hard on women, he reckoned. None loitered outside to smoke with the men.

He had begun to think Dee had given him wrong information until he noticed a change in the tide of humanity washing up against the shore of the church.

The wretches of addiction wandered off, some alone, but mostly in groups of two or three, and as they did, a new wave filled their ranks the same way until a single group of men and women, about a dozen in all, stood near the side entrance of the church. This group wore not the haunted looks of the addicts, but a facade of normalcy to hide that which haunted them. And unlike the previous group, these men and women looked healthy—at least physically—and for the most part, employed, from the painter in splotched coveralls with flecks of dark paint in his white beard to the woman in a dark-green business suit, heels, and expensive leather bag hanging from her shoulder.

Rhonda Raines came into view fifteen minutes before the meeting was to begin. He recognized her immediately. Dee had been thorough and exceedingly efficient, especially considering he was a young black man in an alien and very white small town. He made a mental note to pass the boy an extra hundred.

Rhonda Raines, midforties, divorced, never remarried. Only child, Clifford, shot to death last year. The murder was investigated by her longtime friend and sheriff, Colt Harper. Dee reported that some people suggested Harper and Raines had been much more than friends when they were young.

Rhonda strode past two men puffing on cigarettes with confidence and a smile. A little guarded maybe, but a smile nonetheless, and with far more vivacity than he had anticipated. The grief did not seem to affect her outwardly. And she still had her looks. She wore simple, but not cheap clothes, black pants, white blouse. Gold jewelry and a hint of lipstick.

He watched her disappear into the church. Out of reflex, he checked his watch.

He got out of the car, locked it. He had an hour. Might as well check out the barbecue place he'd passed back up the street.

When he returned, he slipped back into his car just as the meeting broke up. Men and women filed out and stretched their arms, lit cigarettes in the fading daylight, and started or resumed conversations. He watched Rhonda as she made small talk with several women on the sidewalk outside the church. She spoke at length—nearly ten minutes—to one woman in particular, a matronly housewife-looking woman who listened intently. Facial expressions serious, but not grave.

The conversation carried on at such a length that Rhonda was the last person in the area after the housewife woman walked away, toward the center of town.

He met her at her car, coming up from across the street and behind her as she unlocked her door.

"Ms. Raines?" he said, not smiling. He was not a beacon tonight. He was darkness. An unremitting, blank darkness.

She stepped back, drew her breath sharply. Her right hand knifed into her purse.

"Do not," he said. He pulled his blazer back just enough to expose the shoulder holster and the big revolver. "You will come with me. Quietly." He tilted his head toward his car. "This way. In front of me. And trust me, Ms. Raines, I can pull this pistol and shoot you before you can take two steps, if you're considering an escape."

She glared at him. The rage in her eyes, quite the opposite of the fear or pleading or even resignation he expected startled him. She wasn't afraid of him. That mattered not to the darkness. She soon would be.

"Move," he said.

He walked her to the passenger side, opened her door, and she slid in. To any observer, they were a couple going out for a drive in the hazy dusk.

From the small of his back, he produced handcuffs, and before she could react, he had secured her wrists to a U-bolt inside the door. He had installed it specifically for this purpose.

When he was behind the wheel, he looked at her and said, "Do not scream or make any sudden gestures, Ms. Raines."

She stared through the windshield, her jaw muscles working. In the fading light, her profile contrasted sharply against the dark-green foliage outside the window. He was pleased that this was a strong woman.

He drove through town, then took the two-lane road that led back to the rented house. Even though the sun had bled away and the night had come quickly to the clear skies, the day's heat lingered. He ran the air conditioner at high, the fan providing the only sound in the car's interior. Rhonda stared out her window with a fierce countenance, as if plotting his murder.

He swung into the driveway of the rented house, the interior dark and still. Only now did her face betray her fear. This satisfied him.

She began fighting him as soon as he opened her door, even though she was pulled out at an awkward angle. Her flailing legs clipped his a couple of times, and he was surprised at the pain caused by her kicks. She fought with a fury he had rarely seen, in a man or a woman.

She quieted only when he sat astride her back and shoved the muzzle of the revolver into the base of her skull.

He freed her wrists then recuffed her hands behind her back with powerful, deft movements, then hoisted her to her feet and shoved her toward the door.

He pushed her through, ahead of him. Even with the headlights illuminating the interior, the room was soaked in shadows. Rhonda stumbled and fell hard on her side. She groaned, loudly, and scrambled back to her feet. She was quick, like a cat, but it didn't matter. She was merely the mouse, and he the cat.

He stood back and observed her. Her exertions had not tired her. She was sturdy. "Ms. Raines," he said in a level voice, "I will admit these are rather unusual circumstances for introductions, and I hope you'll forgive my coarseness. Unfortunately, my options are limited, as I suppose my invitation would have been rebuffed had I simply asked you to accompany me."

"Who are you?" she said, her voice as level as his.

He reached into a hip pocket and produced a folding knife. A high-tensile serrated steel blade, one of his favorites. Very efficient and extraordinarily effective. He rolled it in the palm of his right hand, enjoying its heft and admiring the potential lethality in such a small instrument.

"That does not matter," he said, his voice low and soothing. "What does matter is that you obey my orders and cooperate fully."

She scoffed, and he felt a flash of anger at her impudence, her defiance of him. He smiled. "Oh, you will, Ms. Raines."

"What do you want from me?" Her eyes shot to the knife in his hand. "I don't have any money."

He took her by the arm and led her to one of the bedrooms in the back of the house. "In due time. What I want has nothing to do with money."

DEE

One thing was for sure: he was tired of white guys. And Mississippi. The whole trip had been a pain in his ass, and he'd be glad to be back in Memphis. Every time there was a bunch of these dumbass rednecks around, somebody got shot. Himself included.

He checked his rearview out of habit, but with the extra concern of knowing the damn car had bullet holes in it. Round here that probably weren't all that unusual, but still, he sure as hell didn't need the heat on his ass.

Hack's comments before he took off to grab the Raines woman still pissed him off. That Delmer motherfucker had it coming, and he didn't regret shooting him one bit. Been his plan all along, soon as he handed over the money. Nobody expected that fool to show up with that sheriff, the one Mr. Freeze was supposed to be killing. How in the fuck *he* showed up there he'd never know.

Hack played it cool, though. Until they got back to the house. There was a second or two when they were sitting in the driveway, sun still not up, when he was sure Hack was going to kill him. But he stayed calm. Well, not calm, but he didn't go apeshit, either.

But that Mexican standoff in that gas station the other day got under Hack's skin, no doubt. He knew Hack was fuming about Harper just sitting there smart-assing him and that cute little lady cop covering him. He was surprised that Hack didn't even try to draw down on the man, but he didn't.

Grabbing that Raines woman, though, that was something. Wanted to do that hisself. That's how he knew Hack was burning up to stick it to Harper good. He would have handled that different, but he wasn't the boss. Still, it pissed him off Hack didn't even bother to send him to do it—even though he threw in an extra hundred for finding her. Instead, he just sent him out here to hand-hold these three idiots.

He headed north on the highway to link up with Strickland, Foster, and Preston. Hack called them "an advantage," but they was really reinforcements. Hack weren't scared of that sheriff, but a blind man could see that the sheriff was trouble—and not one goddam bit scared of Hack, either. He was way too comfortable standing there on that bridge with a pistol on his hip. And especially in that gas station. Fucker didn't even get out of his chair.

That's why he took a shot at that Delmer moron. Shit was getting terminal in a hurry, and he wanted to make sure he got his in before the shit went down. But it went down anyway. He wasn't expecting that sheriff and the brother to be so goddamn fast on the draw.

Truth be told, him and Hack was lucky to get out of there without getting shot all to shit. Hack must have felt it, too, and that's why he called for extra guys.

Strickland and Foster were small-time dumbasses who mostly worked South Memphis and across the Mississippi line. "Collections" is what they called the ass-beatings they handed out to bar owners, dealers, whores, and pimps. Neither of them was very bright and had the rap sheets prove it. They were good with their fists and a gun, though, so they had value to Hack.

Preston, though, was another story. Pure psycho. A lot like Hack, he just realized. Same cold attitude. He heard that Preston once cut a guy's ears off for not listening good enough. Then made the guy talk into his own cut-off hears as a joke before he shot him. Sick shit.

He checked his mirror again, saw only one car behind him—way behind him—and hit his blinker as he rolled into the gravel parking lot of a convenience store—Matt's Mart, the sign said, one of those portable signs with the letters you can put on yourself.

The three men were already there. He recognized Foster's truck. *Why these guys always drive pickup trucks?* he thought as he killed the engine.

He was halfway to the door when it swung open and Strickland came out pulling a big can of beer out of a paper sack. Looking like he'd been working on a car all day. Strickland recognized him and grinned.

The other two followed him, both carrying identical sacks. Foster looked like a less grungy version of Strickland: tall, skinny, loose jeans, Bass Pro T-shirt, baseball cap jammed on top of shaggy blond hair that jutted out from the edges like straw. Preston reminded him of a high school football coach— thick through the shoulders and evenly muscled everywhere else, he was linebacker big in black slacks and a short-sleeve white golf shirt that looked too small. Aviator sunglasses under a coal-black crew cut. You'd never guess he was so handy with a blow torch.

"Yo, Dee, what's up?" Foster called. Strickland popped the top on his beer and raised it to his mouth.

He shrugged. "Not a thing, man. You boys look ready to roll."

Foster nodded. "Hell yeah. But we don't need a guide. You coulda just texted us an address. We all got smart phones."

Strickland snorted around the top of his can. "Hell yeah," he said. "Them phones smarter than we are."

That ain't no shit.

"Yeah, I know," he said, "but Hack was talking about operational security or some shit and told me to make sure I showed y'all how to get there personally."

"Buncha bullshit, you ask me," Foster said.

"Nobody asked you," Preston said. They all turned to this sudden seriousness. "So shut up and drink your fucking beer."

Exactly, he thought.

Preston nodded his head toward the highway. "We should get moving."

"You in a hurry," he said to Preston, who nodded again.

"I am now," Preston said. His head was fixed toward the highway.

He turned and looked over his shoulder. A Chevy, woman driver, was turning in and staring at them. He shrugged. "Yeah, good idea, I guess."

MOLLY

She'd been on her way to her latest hotel room after filling the tank on her car when she noticed the Ford Taurus. Tennessee plates, same numbers she'd memorized and run after the encounter with Hack at the convenience store. She didn't bother to tell Harper—she refused to think of him as "Colt" even though he'd told her to call him that instead of "Sheriff"—because she wasn't about to get in another pissing contest with him over jurisdiction. He would have just tried to shut her down anyway, if she'd told him she was going to run the plates and go after Hack and the kid with him.

This kid—young black male driver—was in front of her, and it made her "Spidey sense" kick in. She'd swung around and followed at a distance for a few miles, eyes fixed on the broken taillight—Harper said he'd shot one out. And she couldn't tell from this distance, but she thought she could make out a bullet hole in the trunk. She fell back on the highway, given the light traffic.

She had a second of self-doubt, picked up her phone to call Harper, but thought better of it. They definitely had different agendas on this one.

The Ford pulled off the highway into the parking lot of a beat-up little building that served as a general store. She tapped the accelerator just enough to close the distance without looking obvious.

She wheeled into the lot and saw the driver standing in front of three men—white men—all of whom looked like standard blue-collar locals. Which confirmed her hunch. The driver was the same kid who was with Hack in the store the day before. He tried hard to look big city. Dope dealer big city, with the oversized Raiders jersey and red ball cap, zirconium rock in his ear and three-hundred-dollar sneakers. All four were smiling like they knew one another and one, the greasy-looking one in crusty jeans and stained short-sleeve shirt, was working on a tall boy. In broad daylight. She could think of absolutely no reason for the Taurus driver to know these guys. So much for him being alone. And too late to call Harper now.

They all stared as she parked and killed the engine.

She climbed out of the car, stood by the hood and stared back across the thirty feet or so of gravel. Shielded her eyes from the glare with her left hand, a neutral look on her face.

"One of y'all drive that Ford?" she called.

The driver snickered. The beefy one, on the far right, frowned. Trouble.

The driver nodded. "Yeah, baby, I do. Why you need to know?"

She shrugged. "Taillight's busted. Thought you might want to know."

Driver laughed. "You gone write me a ticket?"

She lowered her hand. "No, but I would like a word, in private."

That got their attention.

The beefy one looked agitated and moved his hand toward his back.

"Don't do that," she said, but he was already pulling an automatic into view.

Everything happened at once: the Taurus driver yelled and darted toward the store entrance; the beefy one was fast, but she was faster and fired her Sig Sauer twice, hitting him in the throat and chest as he fired at her. The shot went high over her head even as she swiveled to her left to cover the other two. The beer drinker was hauling ass toward a pickup truck on the other side of the parking lot, and the other guy, the tall one, stood facing her, feet apart and both hands wrapped around a revolver. She saw his eyes and felt a hammer blow on the side of her head. She went down on her right side, the wind knocked out of her and the world spinning. She couldn't hear and saw the world turning red, then realized blood was pouring into her eyes. She grabbed her head with one hand and fired three wild shots. She had no idea what she hit. The Taurus driver bolted out of the store, gaped at her, then pushed the shooter out of her field of view.

She passed out for a second and came to, hearing the sound of a vehicle, a truck, roaring away, the drone of the engine fading fast. She rolled onto her back and tried to clear the cobwebs.

She was hurt bad, she knew. She could barely think, but she pushed herself to her knees, then to her feet and staggered to her car. She threw her weapon on the front seat and grabbed her phone. It seemed to take hours to figure out how to use it, and she had to wipe blood off her hands and the phone. She finally mashed the button.

He picked up on the second ring, and she was glad.

"Colt," she said. "I've been shot."

"Where?"

"In the head." She slumped against the car, which felt like it was moving away from her.

"OK," Harper said. "But what I meant was what is your location?"

"Oh, sorry." she said. She mumbled a description of the store as the phone slid from her hand.

Goddamn, it's hot, she thought as she slid down the side of the car, coming to rest against the front tire, her legs straight out in front of her and a terrifying blackness rushing at her.

HACK

He eased open the door to the back bedroom and peered in. Rhonda Raines sprang from the bed but stopped cold at the sight of the revolver in his hand. Her demeanor showed strength, but that strength was betrayed by the fear in her eyes. And as long as she showed fear, he maintained the control he needed.

"You will come with me," he said, opening the door wide and standing aside to let her pass. She walked by, chin slightly raised. "Down the hall to the kitchen," he said.

"Sit," he said when they reached the table. He pulled two cups from a cabinet and filled both with coffee from a pot that steamed and hissed from the counter by the sink. "Sugar? Milk?" he asked.

She shook her head, one defiant shake. He smiled and sat a cup in front of her, then sat opposite her.

She shot him a look, half defiance, half curiosity.

"I have no intention of killing you, if that is a concern of yours," he said. "That is, if I don't have to."

She scoffed. "If you don't have to. What kind of simpleton do you take me for?"

He let that pass and nodded. "There is a larger purpose for which you were selected."

She cocked her head, and her brow furrowed. "What are you talking about, purpose? And selected?"

He drummed his fingers on the oak tabletop. Her obliqueness was a burden. Yet, she did serve a purpose. He cleared his throat, mostly for effect. "As I said, you have a purpose. And that's all you need to know. I now need you to accomplish a simple task for me."

"And what would that task be?"

He did not expect her insolence. Clearly, she felt herself to be his equal. The very thought angered him.

She stared at him with eyes that in any other person would have made him think of himself as prey and raised her cup to her lips.

"You are going to call your former boyfriend and arrange for him to meet me here."

"What?" Her voice ricocheted off the kitchen walls. She sat the cup on the table hard enough to launch a globule of coffee that arced, like a large brown teardrop, halfway across the table and landed in a Rorschach pattern on the light-colored wood.

"I believe I spoke clearly," he said.

"Boyfriend? I don't have a boyfriend, old or otherwise."

"Come now, Ms. Raines, in a small town such as yours your dalliances with certain law enforcement officials does not go unnoticed."

"What?" She narrowed her eyes at him. "You mean Colt?"

He nodded.

She laughed. Further angering him. "You're not from around here, are you? Colt is not my boyfriend. Never was. My word, you been listening to the wrong people."

"Ms. Raines, I advise you to not be evasive," he said, trying not to grit his teeth.

"Had you been listening to the right people," she continued, apparently undeterred, "we wouldn't be having this conversation because you would know that Colt, besides being the best friend I've ever had, always has my back."

He smiled. "Precisely. And it is that status, romantic or otherwise, that I will exploit."

"In what way?"

"You will speak to him on my behalf."

"What for?"

He slid his hand off the table to the holster under his jacket. "Again, you don't need to know. All you need to do is call him, give him your location, and convince him to come here."

"Why?" she said. She looked confused, and he knew she was. "And how am I supposed to convince him to come to…to wherever we are?"

He pulled his revolver and pointed it at her face across the table. Her eyes went wide, and she froze. But her eyes still blazed.

"Tell him I'm holding you at gunpoint."

COLT

I t took John and him about ten minutes to get to the store, and the only conversation en route consisted of John saying, "Hell of a way to run a reelection campaign, boss."

He shot John a glance. "To hell with reelection. I didn't want the job anymore anyway."

"Yeah, I kinda gathered that," John said.

He grunted and hunched over the steering wheel when he saw the sign for Matt's Mart. He was going a little too fast, and the truck slued into the parking lot, slinging gravel toward the storefront. He hit the brakes and threw the gearshift into park. He and John were on the ground and moving almost before the truck came to a stop.

McDonough was sitting against the front tire on the driver's side. At least he thought it was her. Her face was obscured by a silver-haired man squatting in front of her, fussing with what looked like a field dressing.

"Hey," he called as he and John trotted over.

The old guy jerked his head around. His face was red and his crystal-blue eyes glittered in an intense scowl, like an angry clown mask. "Gunshot wound," the old man called out. "I got the bleeding stopped but she's in shock."

He stooped over to get a closer look at both the old guy and McDonough. The old man threw up a forearm to block him.

"Watch it, got dam it," the old man said. "I said she's in shock. EMTs are on the way, but I need to keep her stabilized."

He stood straight, looked at John, who shrugged. And grinned. Just barely.

"Who the fuck are you?" he said.

The old man snorted but didn't even turn his head. His full attention was focused on the blood-soaked compress that he held against McDonough's head. Her eyes were closed, and blood was smeared across her face. He couldn't tell how bad her wound was.

"George Giles," the old man said. "I own this place. I also did a tour in Vietnam as a navy corpsman at Khe Sanh, taking care of Marines. So I know what I'm doing. And who the fuck are *you*?"

"The sheriff and an, uh, acquaintance," he said, a little surprised at Giles's ferocity.

"Mmmmhmmm, so she's a cop?" Giles said to him.

"What makes you think that?"

Giles's laugh sounded like a phlegm-filled bark. "Well, hell's bells, son, she's packing a compact nine-mil in a fast-draw holster," he said. "Plus, she's got a badge that very clearly says 'A-T-F' on it."

John snickered behind him. "Well, goddamn, Doc, get some," he said.

Giles turned his head and cocked an eyebrow at John, an acknowledgment.

He sighed, rather than scream at the old fart. "So, Doc, what's the situation?"

"She took a nine-millimeter slug to the side of her head," Giles said. "It only grazed her skull, but it grazed the shit out of her. She's got a three-inch avulsion—a gash—under this dressing. Knocked her silly, as you can imagine. She's disoriented and lost a lot of blood, but I think she'll be fine. Breathing is shallow, pulse is rapid but strong. She's going to need stitches, and she's gonna have a hell of a concussion."

He nodded, impressed. "Thanks," he said. He felt a rush of relief he couldn't explain, other than McDonough was a cop, too. "You see anything?"

"Oh, hell yeah, I saw the whole thing," Giles said. "They was three of them in my store, all buying beer when this little gang-banger pulled up." Giles cut his eyes at John, who stood as passive as a statue. "Then the three guys walk out and start talking to him—he was a kid, really."

He held up a hand to stop Giles. "These three guys. What did they look like?"

Giles described each of them, noting they were white but not local. "Yeah, it seemed weird to me," he said. "Then she rolled in." He gestured at McDonough with his free hand. "I couldn't hear the conversation, but before you know it, the one guy pulls a gun and all hell breaks loose."

"Which one pulled a gun?" John asked.

"The dead one right over there by the door," Giles said.

He and John turned and noticed for the first time the body of a man laid out in the shade of the storefront, on his back, arms spread in a pool of dark blood."

"No shit," John said.

He noticed McDonough's hand twitch, then flutter toward her head. She mumbled something, and Giles put one hand on her shoulder and the other against the compress. McDonough groaned and tried to push away his hand.

"Hey, there, now, you stop that," Giles said.

"Get off me, goddammit," McDonough said.

"That'll be enough of that," Giles said.

He stared at the dead man. "Who shot him?" he asked.

Giles snorted. "Well, hell, she did. Some of the damnedest shooting I ever seen, I'll tell you that. That dipshit over there had already pulled his piece out, and she still managed to draw down on him and put two rounds through him. This little girl is fast."

He nodded and looked from the dead guy back to McDonough. "So who shot her?"

"One of the other guys," Giles said. "He stood there by the door, too, like he was on the range, two hands on his weapon and fired a shot at her before the black kid pushed him toward the truck they rode up in. Then they hauled ass out of here."

He nodded again. "And that's it?"

"What else do you want? An explosion?" He fussed over McDonough some, even as she struggled against him with profane protests and claims of being "fine, goddammit."

"Fair enough," he said. "I'm going to go check on the dipshit."

"Ahite," Giles said. "I'm sure that sumbitch is still dead."

HACK

ncredulous. If he were asked to describe his reaction to what Dee had just told him, with Strickland and Foster nodding behind him, it would be *incredulous.*

He glared at the three of them standing in the kitchen like little boys who just confessed to knocking out a neighbor's window with an errant baseball.

"And Preston is dead?" he said. "You're sure of that?"

Dee nodded. "I know what dead looks like. That chick smoked him good."

"That...*chick*, as you call her, is in all likelihood a detective."

"That's what I figured."

He continued to stare, not so much at them as his own thoughts. He could already feel repercussions that he'd face in Memphis over this fiasco. If he were ever allowed back in Memphis. This was Knoxville all over again, even though he'd sworn to himself that Knoxville had been an isolated mistake, an aberration. Brooks would not see it that way, of course. Not at all. A sudden feeling of loss rushed at him and made him uncomfortable in its unfamiliarity. At best, the future that loomed was one of exile in obscurity and poverty, and the prospect of it stabbed him with the memory of the life he had left in Kentucky. The certainty of avoiding such a future, which he had felt just a few days ago, evaporated in the kitchen and caused his entire body to shudder. It left him light-headed. He had become accustomed to a lifestyle of power, gratification, and a certain affluence, however ill-gotten. His reputation fed his own self-image and fueled his desires. All that—indeed, his very existence—now lay in jeopardy. His only possible solution was complete the task at hand, regardless of the outcome.

Lashing out at these imbeciles would serve no purpose. His was a solvable problem. He considered himself a professional, and he would behave as one.

He focused on Dee, who wore a thin sheen of perspiration across his mahogany face.

"Is the woman dead?" he asked.

Dee shrugged. "Ain't got no idea. We hauled ass outta there as fast as we could. She was shot in the head, though." Strickland and Foster nodded in unison.

He looked up to the ceiling and back at Dee. "It doesn't matter," he said. "We are about to bring this situation to a resolution. With one Sheriff Colt Harper."

Dee looked at him, his eyes a question. "Yes, Dee, Harper. He has always been a target, even after this idiot Delmer Blackburn decided to become an entrepreneur. And he is still my target. The fates have delivered him to me under the most unlikely of circumstances, but circumstances that I will take full advantage of."

He looked past Dee to Strickland and Foster. "You two," he said, pointing. "You are to be posted outside where you can maintain complete surveillance of the road running in front of the house. Dee, you stay inside with me."

Strickland stuck a finger in the air, like a fifth-grader about to ask a question in class. "Uh, Mr. Hack, what are we looking for?"

"For a vehicle," he said, keeping voice level. "In it will be this sheriff to whom I'm referring, who may possibly be traveling with a large black man. Both of them will be armed. So you should be, as well. When he arrives, I will deal with him personally."

Strickland's face took on a pained look. He nodded at him to ask the question on his mind.

"So, when this sheriff gets here, we do what?"

He smiled. This man was not going to win an award for logic. "You convince him that it will be in his best interest to relieve himself of his weapon. I will take care of the rest."

Strickland nodded as if he understood, though his expression left doubt that he did.

Dee cleared his throat. "How do you know Harper is going to come here? Does he even know where we are?"

He cut his eyes over to Dee. "You let me worry about that. You just follow orders."

Dee nodded, then turned to the other two. "You heard the man," he said. "Get your asses outside."

He watched them file out of the kitchen like obedient pupils, then he walked down the hall and opened the door to the room that held Rhonda Raines.

COLT

He squatted over the corpse and examined the man's clothing. He wasn't dressed like a thug or a dealer or anything, really. He looked like a normal guy, golf shirt, aviator sunglasses. Two entry wounds, one in the upper chest, just missing the heart, the other dead center of the throat. The pulpy wound made him wince more than the wide circle of blood staining the golf shirt. Taking one in the throat had to hurt like a bitch.

From the look of it, the guy fell straight back, arms thrown out. A Glock 19 lay a few inches from the outstretched fingers of his right hand. He scanned the gravel around the body, located one spent shell. That had to be the round fired at McDonough, the one that missed.

He slid his hand under the body and yanked out a wallet, flipped it open. Daniel Preston, thirty-seven, Tennessee license, Memphis address. One credit card. Six hundred eleven dollars in cash. No photos. He closed the wallet and replaced it.

He stood and walked to the spot where Giles said the other shooter stood. No brass in the gravel.

"Hey," he called over his shoulder. "Mr. Giles. You see what the shooter, the one shot her, was carrying?"

"No, I did not."

He nodded, then turned and faced McDonough. Giles was standing, as was McDonough. She wobbled and pushed and argued, and Giles kept leaning on her. Under other circumstances, it would have been funny. She was bleeding like a stuck pig, but at least she was conscious.

He eyeballed the distance from her to the body. About ten yards. A fairly easy shot. But Preston missed, maybe because he was being shot himself. For McDonough, though, that's a very feasible shot. This guy, though, if he was calm like Giles said, couldn't shoot for shit, otherwise McDonough would be dead.

But why was this meeting between these guys even happening? And what the hell was McDonough doing out here alone? The black male had to be the same one from the bridge, the one Delmer called Dee, but how did she come to be following him?

He walked back to John and Giles. "She OK?" he asked. Giles frowned.

"I'm fine, Harper," McDonough said. He looked in her eyes. She couldn't stay focused for very long, but she was coherent. Weak, but coherent."

"You're not fine," he said. "You got shot in the head. You need to go to the hospital."

"Fuck that," she said. "I'm fine."

"Colt," John said, "ambulance is on the way. You sure we want to—"

His cell phone rang from inside his pocket. He held up a hand while he dug it out and looked at the screen: RHONDA.

"What the fuck?" he said, more to himself than anyone else.

"Say again?" John said.

He showed John the phone. John's eyebrows shot up.

He turned away and answered the call. "Rhonda?"

"Hey, Colt, yeah, it's me," she said.

He stared at the store, at Preston lying dead on the shaded gravel, tried to sort out a clash of surprise, anger, and confusion.

"Hey, Rhonda, I don't want to sound rude," he said, "but I'm sort of in the middle of something right now. Is this something that can wait?"

"Colt, listen, OK? I need you to listen to me real careful."

Her voice sounded strained, and an alarm pinged inside his head.

"Go on."

"I need you to come to where I am," she said, her voice quavering. "You know that guy you ran into on the bridge? The one who calls himself Hack?"

"Yeah. Wait, what do you know about that?"

"Doesn't matter. He wants you to come here, with the money you owe him."

"The hell you talking about, Rhonda? I don't owe him shit. He means the money Delmer stole, which he thinks is his."

"Dammit, Colt, shut up and listen," she said. "He is holding a gun on me right now. He wants you to come here alone, with the money, or he will kill me. And, Colt, he's serious."

He glanced over at John, who was chatting with Giles. Off in distance, down the highway he'd driven to get here, he could barely hear an ambulance.

"Rhonda, listen to me. This guy is bad news. He kills people for a living. Do whatever he says. Where are you?"

She rattled off an address, and he made her say it again so he would remember it. "OK," he said, "anything else?"

A pause.

"Yes, Sheriff," Hack said. "There is one more thing. You have one hour to get here, alone, with the money that Delmer Blackburn stole from my employer. If you're late by even a minute, I'm going to make your dear friend Mrs. Raines excruciatingly uncomfortable."

He closed his eyes and bowed his head as he felt a curious calm overtake him. He smiled to himself.

"I take it you understand these instructions?" Hack asked.

He cleared his throat. "Fuck you," he said. "I'll see you in an hour." He broke the connection, then punched the address Rhonda had given him into a maps app on his phone.

"Colt?" John asked behind him. He turned to see his deputy wearing a concerned look. "What's up?"

He shook his head. "You're not going to believe this one. Hack has Rhonda. Wants me to meet him in an hour with the money, or he'll kill her."

"What?" John said. "How in the hell did she get involved in this?" He stomped over from McDonough's side, hands on hips, clearly alarmed.

"I have no idea, and it don't matter. What does matter is putting this sumbitch down."

John nodded. "Right. Let's go."

He shook his head. "He said alone."

"That's bullshit, Colt, and you know it. I'm going with you."

"No, goddammit, you're not," Colt said, already walking to his truck. He stopped and turned. "Look, John, I know you and Rhonda have something. I respect that. Hell, I'm glad for it. And that's exactly the reason I don't need you going. I'm going to put this guy down, and that's going to be the end of it."

"Is it?" John said, clearly angry.

"Yeah, John, it is. I have to go."

"What you want me to tell the cops and the EMTs and everybody else that's going to show up asking a shitload of questions?"

He sighed. "Right now, John, I don't give a fuck. Tell them whatever you want. Tell them we're part of a special task force or some bullshit. Or it's all part of an ongoing investigation. I'll deal with all this later." He turned again and climbed into his truck.

He spun the truck around, throwing gravel and squealing the tires when he hit pavement. In his rearview mirror, he saw McDonough waving her arms and pushing John while Giles did his best restrain her. John could handle that, and he felt pretty sure Giles had taken good care of McDonough. It was out of his hands now, anyway.

He was doing seventy a couple of minutes later when he met the ambulance roaring up the road, lights and sirens going full tilt. A brown-and-white sheriff's car followed behind, blue lights going.

He hit the brakes too hard in the sheriff's department parking lot, and his truck slid on the pavement almost into the side of the building. He ran inside, yelled at Becky for the key to the evidence locker and was roaring down the highway with the money on the seat beside him in less than five minutes.

His mind raced, sorting courses of action, but John's voice still rang in his ears, a snarling question that sounded like an accusation: "Is it?"

HACK

He holstered the pistol and smiled at Rhonda. Her brown eyes blazed back at him. She seemed genuinely frightened on the phone, but now, sitting on the edge of the bed in her work clothes with her legs crossed and arms folded across her chest, she seemed anything but. Her mouth was a compressed line across her face, and her eyes gleamed with fury. He found her visage amusing and curious. She was either too stupid to realize that she would soon be dead or delusional enough to believe that the bravado she was displaying would keep her alive. His instinct told him the latter, but it was of no consequence to him. That bravado would soon serve to gratify him immensely as he slowly demonstrated the reality of his power to her.

"You're going to regret this," she said to him in a voice devoid of the apprehension of just a few minutes ago.

He smiled. "I'm sure you believe so. However, I don't share that belief."

"You're an arrogant man."

He scoffed. "Arrogant. Only because you don't believe me."

She crossed her arms and opened her mouth to speak but clamped her mouth shut.

"Now," he said, "your phone. Give it to me."

She arched her eyebrows.

"You don't really think I'm going to give you the chance to warn him, do you? I could hear the intimacy in your voice. Hand it over."

Her eyes flickered, and he thought he saw fear at last, and an electric thrill ran through him. She picked the phone up off the bed and handed it to him.

He nodded. "Good girl. Now, you will stay in this room until I tell you to come out. Is that clear?"

She nodded.

"Good." He left her sitting on the bed and closed the door behind him. He walked to the window in the living room and peered out at Strickland and Foster. Strickland held a sawed-off twelve-gauge and stared down the road to the left. Foster, wearing his revolver on his right hip, watched to the right. He checked his watch—fifty more minutes. He heard the clicking of bullets into a magazine coming from the kitchen where Dee was preparing for battle.

He smiled through the window. He could be back in Memphis by tomorrow.

COLT

He could end this right now, he knew, just call for backup and stand this guy off. By the book.

He could do that. Except for the fact that it was Rhonda being held hostage. And he couldn't abide that.

But most of all, the thought as he climbed into the truck and turned the ignition key, *most of all*, Hack was after *him*. Had been from the beginning. Delmer just got in the way of that. Delmer's actions, and his whole connection to him, had been a collision of fates, a bizarre confluence of lives never meant to intersect, but it did not diminish the fact that Hack was after him and sooner or later they would meet again, likely with fatal results. So it might as well be sooner.

He didn't believe in destiny, but he knew the confrontation ahead of him had been ordained, and there was no escaping that, any more than he could escape the past. There was no light at the end of the tunnel, no Promised Land lying below the mountaintop. He walked through the valley of the shadow alone and with a gun because at the end of the valley there was usually another man with a gun. That's all there was to it.

He pulled out onto the highway, checked his watch. His phone map indicated the route with a blue line, and he followed its instruction. He reached over to the glove compartment and pulled out his Glock, leaned over the steering wheel and jammed the boxy pistol in the small of his back, left side, as his phone told him to turn right. He swung into the turn onto a macadam road as the phone told him his destination was 3.1 miles ahead on the left.

He peered ahead, seeing only the gray strip of pavement, soybean field on the left, small white ranch house on the right. A flash in his mirror jerked his eyes up. About five car lengths behind him, a dark sedan was keeping pace with him, even though he was up over seventy-five miles an hour. He squinted at the mirror and realized the driver was McDonough.

Has she lost her fucking mind? Other than taking a bullet through it?

He frowned, considered his options, even as he sped toward Rhonda's location. Pulling over and arguing with a wounded, half-crazed in-shock federal agent did nothing to help his predicament. And running her off the road would certainly do nothing to help hers. He shook his head and pressed the accelerator. He only had one option, the original one: get to Rhonda as fast as he could.

He took one last glance at the mirror, then focused his attention on the road ahead of him.

Then he saw it. Or, rather, him.

His truck barreled toward a man—white, scruffy, even from a distance—holding a sawed-off shotgun. Staring up the road at him. Beyond the man, now in full view, another male, also white, facing the opposite direction. Sentries. Second man unarmed, apparently.

He floored it, and the truck leapt forward like an attack dog unleashed. The far man spun around, and he saw that man draw a pistol from his hip. He had the random thought that he would have already shot out the tires, had he been the sentry on duty. He gripped the wheel with both hands, then jammed the brakes and jerked the wheel hard to the right, causing the truck to shudder and fishtail from the pavement toward the low ditch separating him from the two sentries. As the truck swung past ninety degrees, he rammed the gear shift to park, flung open the door, and leaped from the cab in one huge movement.

The closest man held his shotgun at his hip, leveled at him. He did not seem afraid.

He moved to his right to put the shotgun between him and the pistol sentry, about fifteen yards distant.

He yanked out both pistols, Glock in his left, .45 in his right, and leveled the .45 at the closer man and fired just as the man realized what was happening and pulled the trigger on his shotgun.

He saw the man fly backward as the bullet hit him in the chest at the same time he felt a sledgehammer blow to his right leg. He spun, nearly lost his balance, and regained his footing as the pistol shooter drew a bead on him. He fired the Glock twice and saw the man twitch, then shudder as a wide bloodstain appeared in his shirt, up high near the left shoulder. The man fired, and he felt another fist of fire and pain slam into him on his left side, in the ribs. The shot staggered him, and he stumbled toward the first gunman, who lay facedown over his shotgun.

Goddam that hurts, he thought as he fought to stay upright. Blood poured freely down his right leg and from a ragged wound in his left side. He had trouble breathing and gritted his teeth against the pain. He saw the pistol shooter reel and sink to one knee, then raise his revolver again.

Behind him, brakes squealed. Then McDonough's voice; "Harper!" He jerked his head to see her fire her weapon at the pistol shooter, missing twice.

He adjusted, fired the Glock twice more, this time hitting the shooter both times, once in the chest and once in the head. The man flew backward in a spray of blood and fell to one side, dead.

To his right, he heard the unmistakable sound of shotgun being racked. He swung around, astonished the man was still alive. He had pulled himself up on his elbows, but his fish-belly white face bobbed like a yo-yo as he bled out. Yet, he fired the shotgun again, the buckshot going wide, but close enough to find flesh, this time in his lower left leg.

His brain felt like it short-circuited from this new pain. He gasped and forced himself to level his .45, even as his assailant racked yet another shell. From somewhere very close behind him, McDonough's weapon roared. He winced at the shock to his ears as McDonough shot the man through the top of the head, killing him, and fired once more into the man's body.

He stumbled backward into McDonough and lowered his arms. She grunted and pushed him upright. With an effort that instantly exhausted him, he looked over his shoulder. Her eyes were glazed and unfocused. Her pistol smoked at her side. She licked her lips once and said, "Go," a croak she punctuated with a nod. His breath heaved in and out of his chest. McDonough, still nodding, sank to her knees like an imploding skyscraper and crumpled face-first onto the grass.

Unsure if he could walk, he leaned forward. The house loomed in front of him. Rhonda must be in there. He felt light-headed, from blood loss, he knew. He took small steps toward the house. The door flew open and smacked the brick exterior with a crack that sounded like another gunshot to his numb ears.

Hack stepped through the door onto a small, low wooden deck that served as a porch. He shoved Rhonda ahead of him, left arm wrapped around her throat, gun in his right hand held to her head. The skinny black kid, Dee, slithered past him on the right.

He blinked back the pain and raised both pistols.

Hack smiled down on him. "I see you met Strickland and Foster," he said, his voice carrying a tinge of respect.

It hurt to breathe, much less talk. "Those idiots couldn't shoot for shit," he said.

He locked eyes with Rhonda. Her face was a mask of dark fury. If Hack had expected her to be afraid, he had been wrong. She stood still, hands at her sides, but she fumed under Hack's grip.

"Their orders were to get you to me alive," Hack said. The irritating smile never wavered. "They succeeded, barely. Here you are. A little worse for wear, but here nonetheless."

Another wave of pain rolled over him, and he let out a stifled groan. He saw Dee slide to the right, eyes on him like a cat.

He raised the .45 an inch. "Take one more step and I'll kill you," he said. Dee stopped moving.

Hack continued to talk. "You know how this is going to end, Sheriff Harper. Why delay the inevitable? Do you hope to bleed to death before I kill you?"

He gritted his teeth. "You are an obnoxious son of a bitch, you know that? I'm not some backwoods dope dealer running scared of you."

Dee slid one foot forward, and he leveled the .45 and shot the kid in the head. The slug slammed Dee against the brick with a sound exactly like that of a watermelon being dropped on a sidewalk. Hack's eyes widened for a split second, whether in horror or surprise he couldn't tell. But that goddamn smile was gone.

He leveled the .45 at Hack and, though he didn't want to look weak, he lowered his left arm to the wound in his side.

"Let her go," he said, his breath wheezing.

Hack scoffed.

He met Rhonda's eyes, and she held his gaze, a desperate attempt to communicate. She stared at him until he understood what she was asking, and she blinked once, slow and deliberate. And he understood. Then she twitched her hip and swung her right arm up and back, aiming for Hack's crotch.

Her sudden movement distracted Hack for a fraction of a second—all the time in the world. Hack jerked downward and tried to pull Rhonda straight by the neck.

He squeezed the trigger and shot Hack just over his right eyebrow. The .45 slug blew out the back of his head and drove his dead body back through the open door. His grip slid from Rhonda as he fell into the interior of the house, and she dropped to her knees, gasping for air.

His body went weak from blood loss, pain, and the adrenaline rush. He sank slowly to his knees, still holding the pistols, his breath ragged gasps. He gulped for more air as he settled into the grass, his head spinning and his ears ringing. He heard his mother's voice, faint and barely discernible, singing a song he couldn't quite name, though the melody was familiar. Then he remembered and smiled, for he understood that, in this moment, he was most assuredly leaning on the everlasting arms.

A blackness rushed upon him. He closed his eyes and fell face-first to the ground.

EPILOGUE

Beeping. Cold beeping, very cold beeping. *Wait, sounds ain't cold. What the fuck is so cold?*

His eyes fluttered open and were stabbed by the harsh fluorescent lights in the ceiling. White light. White everything.

Oh yeah, I got shot. Apparently made it to a hospital. Somewhere. Where the hell am I? And why is this room so damn cold?

He turned his head to the right: IV stand, a huge tangle of tubes running from all sorts of panels by the bed and into him. Window with green curtains, drawn.

He swiveled the opposite direction, toward the beeping, which came from the machine by the head of the bed. LED display of numbers he couldn't comprehend. Behind the machine, in a chair, a mop of hair. Reddish. The hair moved, and McDonough looked up, green eyes tired and a huge bandage on the side of her head. She was too good-looking to look ridiculous, but she almost did.

Shit, did I say that out loud?

"Say *what* out loud?" McDonough asked.

His mouth was sandpaper-dry. "Nothing," he croaked. "How long—"

"Most of a day," she said. "Doc says you're going to be in a lot of pain and very weak for a while."

"Doc was right."

"Yeah, and that's even with all the morphine they shot you up with."

"Thank God for morphine. How 'bout you?"

She shrugged and stood. Still in jeans and a ratty T-shirt, ponytail. "I'm OK. A headache that would kill a lumberjack and some stitches, but I'm OK."

He nodded and stared at the ceiling. "You should learn to stay out of the way of bullets."

She smirked. "Said the man shot three times."

He smiled, even though doing so caused a stab of pain in his side. "Hey, one of those doesn't count—he only grazed me."

"Yeah, well, you're the one in the hospital bed."

"Fair enough."

"I'll get a nurse," McDonough said and turned toward the door.

"Wait," he said through a cough. "Can you get me some water?"

McDonough poured him a plastic cup full from the small aluminum pitcher on a stand at this bedside. He drank it down, and he realized he was so high from the painkillers he could hardly think straight.

"Where's Rhonda and John?" he asked.

McDonough's face turned serious. "Rhonda is downstairs, worried sick about you. She wants to see you, though. John's with her."

"Good." He squinted at her. "How did you manage to get away from John?"

She winced and looked ashamed. "I pulled my weapon on him."

"That's pretty crazy."

"Seemed like a good idea at the time."

He shook his head. "You could have gotten yourself killed."

"Look who's talking," she said.

He turned to look at her. "I owe you one," he said.

She crossed her arms, brow furrowed. "You don't owe me shit, Harper. You would have done the same thing."

"But... "

"Look, Colt," she said, her voice low, "that guy had to go down, and if I couldn't be the one to do it, I sure as hell wasn't going to let you do it alone. Simple as that."

He locked eyes with her. She was strong, but behind the steady gaze he saw a softness that had not been evident before.

"OK, Molly." He closed his eyes. "I guess I fucked up your chance at redemption, huh?"

She stared down at him long enough to make him uncomfortable under her gaze. She shook her head. "You killed that son of a bitch. That'll have to be redemption enough. For both of us."

He stared back at her. Maybe she was right. He would think about it some more when he wasn't so tired.

"What about you, though?" he asked. "You must be in the doghouse with your boss."

She shrugged again. "I resigned. Only thing left for me to do. Like I said, redemption enough."

He drew a painful breath, let it out. "I'm sorry about that."

"Don't be. I'm not." She moved away from the bed. "I'll get the nurse."

He closed his eyes and nodded. He stared at the ceiling and tried to force his mind to think of something other than the fact that he was, in all likelihood, soon to be out of a job, even though he knew he didn't want the job anymore. He marveled at his wounded pride, even through the painkillers.

He heard a very faint click, and the door to his room opened. He rolled his head to the left as Rhonda glided in, her face grim.

He tried to smile, and it must have worked, because she managed a weak smile in return. Her eyes shone in the low light of the room, and she took his hand at the bedside.

His lips felt dry again, but his eyes were stinging, for some reason. He blinked until he could see her clearly.

"Rhonda," he said with a voice that sounded to him like a growl. "I'm sorry about all this. Are you OK?"

She closed her eyes for a long second, and twin pendants of tears glistened down her cheeks. She nodded, finally, and looked at him with eyes brimming. "You're something else, Colt Harper," she said, her voice barely more than a whisper. She tried to laugh, but it came out a gasp. "You're laying here all shot to pieces and you're asking me if I'm OK. Yes, all things considered, I'm fine."

He nodded and lay back on his pillow, exhausted. He stroked her hand with his thumb.

"Thank you," he said.

She wiped her eyes. "For what?"

"For having faith in me with that shot."

More tears. "I was terrified, Colt. I was sure we were going to die."

"Then…why?"

She sighed. "Because if we were going to die at the hands of that…that monster, then we were going to go down fighting. I saw that in your eyes, too. And that look in your eyes scared me as much as that man did. Just like it did the very first time I saw it."

She leaned over him and locked eyes with him. "But I trusted you. Of course I did. I always have."

He closed his eyes and felt a wetness on his cheeks.

What did McDonough say? That'll have to be redemption enough.

He opened his eyes and stared at Rhonda, who smiled now for real.

"Thank you," he said.

"You're welcome," she said. "Now get some rest. I'll get the nurse."

He closed his eyes again, and she slipped out of the room. He was asleep long before the nurse arrived.

novel, *Enemy Within*, ". [and] asks some probin abdication of responsibil ing decay of US civil rig *Simple Murder* and *Dee* in *O-Dark-Thirty*; *The [* *Out of the Gutter Onli* *Knuckle*; *Yellow Mama*; the Bread Loaf Writers

He also authored the experience, *Into the Stor*

He lives in Virgini and online at his blog, *wordpress.com*.